RED SKY
AT
MORNING

RED SKY AT MORNING

Andrea Wyman

HOLIDAY HOUSE/NEW YORK

Library of Congress Cataloging-in-Publication Data
Wyman, Andrea.
Red sky at morning / by Andrea Wyman.
p.   cm.
Summary: In Indiana in 1909, Callie finds that she must grow up
quickly when death and other hardships leave her alone
on the family farm with her ailing grandfather Opa.
ISBN 0-8234-0903-1
[1. Farm life—Fiction.   2. Indiana—Fiction.   3. Frontier and
pioneer life—Fiction.   4. Grandfathers—Fiction.]   I. Title.
PZ7.W9788Re   1991   91-55029   CIP   AC
[Fic]—dc20

The writing of this historical novel engaged a number of helpful and enthusiastic people along the way. I would like to thank the Indiana Council for the Humanities for bending the rules to send research materials out-of-state; the Indiana Historical Society's untiring staff of reference librarians; Jane and Everett Foust with their treasure-trove memories; Martha Timmons of the Sheridan Public Library; Heike Koenig for sharing a German bedtime story; Eleanor Arnold, Editor, of the series *Memories of Hoosier Homemakers;* Professor Günther Gerlitzki, consultant, on the German sections and Glossary; and Margery Cuyler, for her patience and guidance.

A. W.
April 15, 1991

For Susan, Drew and Rick,
and with loving memories of the real Callie,
my grandmother, Clystie Marie Manship, 1896–1984.

Contents

CHAPTER ONE

Papa's Letter

Perched like a little bird on a stringer of fence wire, I saw cornfield after cornfield after cornfield. Acres and acres of cornfields sprawling along the flat countryside, coloring everything in sight a bright, emerald green. Row after row of green stalks sporting tassels flopped over like trimming on a fancy hat. There was wheat that year, too. Acres of golden wheat fields, dipping and waving in the breeze. Cornfields and wheat fields. Two things I'd come to know like the back of my hand. When my eyes were closed and the wind came up, I imagined I was at the ocean. The wheat fields rolling and rippling like giant ocean waves and the rustling of the cornstalks sounding like water sliding up to shore and splashing against the rocks. Least ways, that was the notion Papa'd given me. The one he'd planted in my head before he left.

*   *   *

"Do you think we'll ever see the ocean?" I asked my sister, Katherine, on that hot day in August. "The P-A-C-I-F-I-C Ocean," I spelled for practice. "Can you see the Pacific Ocean from Oregon?" I wanted to sound like I was some kind of world traveler. But truth to tell was, I'd never been farther than my own backyard in Bakers Corner. Never even out of Hamilton County. Never even out of the state of Indiana. I turned to look at Katherine. I had a feeling she wouldn't answer. Every time I brought up the subject of Oregon, Katherine turned a deaf ear.

"Did you notice how pale Mama looked this morning?" Katherine asked. She was standing barefoot, drying canning jars on the back porch by the pump.

"No, not exactly," I answered. "Don't ladies that are gonna have babies look a little pea-ked sometimes?"

"Better not let Aunt Mary hear you talk about having babies. You know we're not allowed to talk about things like that," Katherine reminded me.

"Aunt Mary's an old goose," I answered. "Besides, Mama looks fine to me. You worry too much. Mama just looks like a lady who's about to have a baby. The only thing that's got me worried is what they're gonna name it. Seems like no one's given the name any thought."

"I think Mama and Papa should name the baby Clement. Clement is a lovely name," Katherine replied. She turned and put the last jar on the table, then headed out toward the clothesline to hang up her dish towel.

"Clement! Oh mercy! That'll sound pretty silly on a girl, if you ask me."

"Well, nobody's asking you, Calista Common. Course nobody has to. You're always giving your opinion on any subject, free as you please," Katherine said as she stuck a clothespin over the dish towel.

We both turned at the same time when we heard a wagon coming up the lane.

"Uncle Mike's here already," I shouted. "Yahoo! He's early today!"

We ran over to the wagon before Uncle Mike completely stopped, scaring the horse a little.

"It's all right, Blick," Katherine said, patting his nose. I kept my distance, but then I always kept my distance when it came to horses.

"How's Blick today?" Katherine asked as though he was going to answer. Katherine pumped a fresh bucket of water for him.

"Uncle Mike, Uncle Mike," I said, scrambling up the side of the wagon to stand on the footrest. "We didn't think you'd be here so early in the day."

"How could I not visit the two prettiest girls on Mule Barn Road on a hot old Saturday afternoon?" he told us. Every Saturday Uncle Mike brought out supplies to our farm on Hollyhock Hill.

With both her hands, Katherine carried the water bucket over to Blick and set it down right under his nose. He curled his thick lips and sucked at the water like he had a straw. Katherine brushed a wisp of hair from her face and wiped the sweat from her forehead with her apron.

Uncle Mike smiled and pushed back his hat. He rubbed his bristly handlebar mustache and scratched the fuzzy sideburns running along his jawline. He was our mother's tall, trim bachelor uncle. To look at him, it was hard to tell that he was Opa's brother. The fifteen years difference in their ages and the difference in their dispositions made them seem like night and day.

Uncle Mike started unloading bundles and dumping feed bags into our arms. We marched into the kitchen, where I jumped on a brightly printed sugar sack and pushed my hand into Uncle Mike's vest pocket.

"Mind your manners, Callie," Aunt Mary said, coming into the room.

"Seems to me, Mary, I brought a treat for the girls," Uncle Mike said, with a grin that showed a wide space between his front teeth. "Only in my old age, I can't rightly remember where I put it!" He scratched his chin and then began pulling on his ear.

"Hmmmm," he muttered, searching his pants pockets. "Well-l ...," he hedged, fumbling through his vest. As he pulled off his hat to scratch his balding head, two sparkling red pieces of wrapped candy clinked to the floor.

I scrambled after the piece that went under the kitchen table and had it in my mouth before I crawled out again.

"Shouldn't be wasting good money on foolishness like candy," Aunt Mary grumbled. We laughed when Uncle Mike held out a dark purple piece, and she took it quickly.

"Grape's my favorite," she said, almost smiling. "I like to try and make candy last a long, long time."

Aunt Mary was a shirttail relative, actually Opa's sister-in-law. We'd always called her Aunt Mary although, in truth, she was our mother's widowed aunt. Aunt Mary and I walked around each other like two cats ready for a fight, but she was different with Mama and Katherine. Aunt Mary had a fondness for Mama, maybe from having only had two sons, Algis and Arza. Katherine had patience with Aunt Mary's ways and seemed to understand why Aunt Mary was always cross and disagreeable.

"Life's been hard on her," Katherine explained.

"Aunt Mary only knows two things, the boarding-house and the boys. That's all she ever really had."

After I thought about that for a while, I guessed I could see why Aunt Mary liked Mama and coming out to the farm to visit. Mama was the sweetest person to be around, and our place was constantly busy with one thing or another. People were stopping by all the time, and we generally had enough work that an extra pair of hands for chores was always welcome.

As I went to hug Uncle Mike around the waist, my leg knocked into the kitchen table.

"Be careful what you're doin' or else skedaddle outside," Aunt Mary told me and Katherine. Mama and Aunt Mary had spent the morning canning. Jars of cooling peaches lined the kitchen table like little soldiers in orange uniforms.

"Thank you," I told Uncle Mike, rolling the sweet cherry chunk from side to side.

Katherine was more polite. She daintily popped the candy into her mouth.

"Where's Elschen?" Uncle Mike asked. "I have this here letter for her. I know for sure she's gonna want to see it right away quick."

"She's gone out on the porch with Opa to sit a spell. There's not been a breath of air anywhere this afternoon."

We followed Aunt Mary through the house. The screen door slapped shut as we tagged along. Mama was sitting in a rocker she'd moved to a shady spot. She was fanning her face with a bamboo fan that read Lechleitner's Dry Goods Store, Main Street, Russiaville, Indiana.

Uncle Mike stood awkwardly over her and took off his hat. Ever since she'd grown big with the baby, Uncle Mike didn't know what to do with himself when he was around her.

"This here came for you today, Elschen," he explained, fishing inside his vest pocket. "And the minute I saw what it was, I thought I'd make a trip out so you could have it."

He handed her a thin letter, then sat down on the edge of the porch, propping himself up against a pillar. He used his hat to fan himself and wiped his neck with a red bandanna.

"Lordie me," said Aunt Mary when she saw what it was.

Mama suddenly did look pale, almost lily-white. She held the letter from Papa for so long I was afraid she wasn't going to open it.

"Don't you want to read it?" I asked. Katherine promptly jabbed me in the ribs with her elbow.

Mama slit the top open with Uncle Mike's pocketknife, and we watched as her eyes scanned the lines.

"Oh, Mama, aren't you gonna read it out loud?" I asked. Katherine popped me in the ribs once more.

"Maybe it's personal and your mama doesn't want to share it," Uncle Mike said.

Papa and the minister's son had gone out to Oregon, hoping to find good, rich farmland to buy. They'd been away two months, but it felt like forever.

Mama looked past us toward the end of the lane.

"Elschen?" he asked, wrinkling his brow as he peered into her face.

Mama stared like she was in a trance, but she snapped out of it and said, "It's all right, Mike. I, uh, well, I simply forgot what I was doing there for a second."

Mama straightened herself in the rocker a bit and cleared her throat. The thin paper wavered ever so slightly as Mama held the letter. She quickly turned it over, then back to the beginning once again.

"It says here at the top, July 10, 1909. This letter surely took a long time getting here, didn't it, girls?" she remarked, looking up briefly. " 'Dear Ones.' " Mama stopped reading and spoke the rest.

"This first part is about how beautiful it is in Oregon. How the rolling hills are always colored with wildflowers, sometimes a light lavender, sometimes a blushing pink." She pointed to the bottom half of the page. "And this part is about how it took Papa so much longer than he thought to get there. 'The traveling went much slower than I expected and we camped one night near Kearney, Nebraska, when our wagon broke down,' " Mama read. Her voice trailed off.

With my chin tucked nicely into the cup made by my palm, my thoughts drifted away as Mama talked of mules and broken wheels. And I thought only of Papa.

It was probably true that I was more Papa's girl than Mama's. At least that's what people were always saying. Just hearing the words he'd written made me miss him so. I thought of his strong hands, first off. Strong leathery hands with thick fingers that could fix anything. Sturdy fingers that would surround mine tightly but so gently and sweetly that it felt like there was an invisible string tied to my heart. Every time Papa's name was mentioned since he'd been gone, that little string got a tug on it.

Maybe I didn't take after the quiet and shy part of Papa, but Katherine and I knew how to bring the laughs out of him. We pulled him down on the parlor rug one time. Katherine held his face to one side, her fists full of beard, while I tickled a spot behind his ears with my fingers. He laughed and hollered and squirmed and laughed some more. My papa had a beautiful laugh that could fill a whole room all by itself.

By the time I looked up at Mama, she was putting the letter back into the envelope. "He sends us his love and wishes he could have us together again as soon as possible. He says his heart is always with us, even though we're apart." The way Mama put Papa's letter back into the envelope, I thought the letter might never come out again.

That moment was when I realized I'd have to get the letter for myself. To see Papa's writing, to read the words, to make sure he was still all right, still real. I wanted to make certain he was surely on his way to a place called Oregon. With Papa gone, there was a big empty hole in my heart. I looked up at Mama.

There were tight lines encircling Mama's mouth. Her lips seemed as thin as two sewing needles. Her left eye started to give a little twitch now and again, and she kept dabbing at her face with a hankie. She was looking so pale and white in that August heat.

Aunt Mary looked from Mama to Uncle Mike, then back to Mama again. "Why don't you rest now, Elschen? It's been such a hectic day. I know you must be tired. Here," she added, stepping forward to take the letter from Mama, "I'll put this on the credenza for you."

"No," Mama nearly hollered. She held the letter with both hands as if she'd never let go of it. "No," she said a little more quietly, "I'll keep it here on my lap."

Aunt Mary patted Mama gently on the shoulder. "No need to fret about the letter, that's fine. You rest now." Aunt Mary turned to shoo us off the porch.

Once we were inside, Katherine asked, "Is Mama all right?"

"Yes, I think so," Aunt Mary said, looking back over her shoulder toward the porch. "But it's been a strain, what with your father leaving the way he did. There was that nasty business about the money, too. He's a dreamer, that one. For months the only thing your papa could talk about was free land out in Oregon. Lord knows, nothing in life is ever free. No one believed him, except your mama. But it looks as though things are gonna take care of themselves. Your mama's been worrying enough for the whole family. He wanted a farm that would look out over the Pacific Ocean. Maybe he's found it after all."

Aunt Mary started us on the job of filling the

woodbox by the stove in the kitchen. "And when that is done, you can go out and get the eggs," she said and went upstairs.

Out by the woodpile, I told Katherine what I wanted to do.

"You'll get your backside whipped if you do a thing like that," she cautioned.

"Not if I don't get caught."

As we spoke, I motioned for her to keep carrying wood to the kitchen and making a lot of noise, like there were two of us doing the job. Then I stole around the side of the house and hid behind the hydrangea bush near the front porch. I was crouched low, but I could see Mama, and I knew from the way her head was drooping that she was fast asleep.

I silently climbed up on the porch and crawled along the floor on my stomach until I was close enough to touch her. My heart was pounding so loud I was almost certain a person could hear it. I clamped one hand over my chest to keep the heart-beats from booming out. Then, careful as you please, I slipped the letter off Mama's lap. When I started backing down, I nearly jumped out of my skin. There was Katherine, standing stock-still beside the house, her mouth hanging wide open. She was staring right at me.

Mama never once moved the whole time. As

Katherine and I ran behind the house and up the hill to the old chicken coop where the hollyhocks grew, we heard the clock on the credenza striking twice.

"Close your mouth before you catch a fly," I told Katherine, since she was still staring at me.

"I can't believe you just did that, Calista Common."

I held the letter up to her face and gave her my best nonchalant look.

"I can read Papa's handwriting easily," Katherine said proudly. We hid ourselves by sitting on the back side of the big old linden tree.

Carefully, I slid the paper out of the envelope and handed it to Katherine.

"Dear Ones," I'd been hearing in my mind ever since Mama first read Papa's letter.

"Go ahead," I said. "You start." Trading the lines, I knew we could read Papa's words to each other, making them sound so much better in our own voices.

Mine was like Papa's, froggy and rough and deep. People always talked about how I resembled Papa. Even down to the sparkle in my eyes.

"That one's got your big, sparkly, blue eyes, Owen," Mr. Comstock told Papa over the counter of the dry goods store one day. Harold Comstock pointed right at me while I stood by the button drawer. Customers in the store turned around.

Before Katherine even started to read, I could hear Papa's perfect pronunciation in her voice. I loved the way Papa always clipped each word as though he had a pair of sewing scissors for a tongue. He and Katherine could snip the ends off "burnt toast" like dangling threads.

Katherine was already reading, silently.

"Hey, what are you doing! You're supposed to be reading aloud. Does he say anything about the Pacific Ocean? Read me the parts about Oregon. The part where he says the fields are so colorful with wildflowers."

"Hush!" Katherine said, giving me an angry look. "Be still for a minute." She stood up suddenly and began walking away, holding the letter.

"What are you doing?" I stood up to follow.

"Shhhh," she said, not looking up from the letter but turning it over to read the back.

The more she read, the darker her face became.

"What is it?" I asked, standing beside her.

She hesitated a minute before answering me.

"It's all a lie," Katherine told me.

"What do you mean, 'it's all a lie'?"

Katherine's arms dropped to her sides and her shoulders sagged.

"It's made up. Mama made it up, just now when she read this to us." Katherine's hand tapped the letter. She looked me straight in the face. "Papa's been swindled."

"Swindled?" I asked. "What's swindled?"

"He's been tricked. Deceived," she said, handing me the letter. "A man swindled him out of his money in St. Louis." She pointed to a paragraph on the front page. "He promised Papa land out in Oregon. Took everything Papa had. Gave Papa a phony bill of sale for land that didn't even exist. Said Papa would have a hundred and fifty acres of farmland on the ocean." Katherine sank to her knees in a heap.

I took the letter and read the words for myself. They didn't have Papa's voice to them the way I'd hoped. They didn't make me feel good and happy inside. They only made me feel numb and empty.

"Oh, poor Papa," I said as I sat next to Katherine. "Poor Mama."

"That money was everything they had," Katherine said. "He had Opa's money, too." Katherine stared out past the old chicken coop toward a field of corn almost ready for picking.

"Why didn't Mama read this to us?" I asked.

"It's my guess she doesn't want anyone to know," Katherine said, looking at me. "We have to keep this a secret. We can't let anyone find out."

"Why not? It's an honest mistake."

"It'll bring a disgrace to the family."

"How's that?"

"Do you remember what happened the night before Papa left?"

"Kind of."

"Do you remember how Papa and Opa got into the argument about the money? Opa saying how he didn't think Papa needed to take all the money. And then the next day, Opa went to look for the money he'd hidden and Papa had taken it anyway."

"Was that what the yelling was about?"

"It sure was. Papa took Opa's money without asking. It was nearly a thousand dollars Opa had buried in a tobacco can out in the barn. Opa even called Papa a Dieb."

"A thief," I cried. "Papa's not a thief. Maybe it can be straightened out in Oregon. Maybe Papa can find the man that took the money and make it all right. I'm positive our papa's not a thief."

"Well, some people would say he's a thief. They'd say worse than that."

Katherine and I both stood up as we faintly heard the clock striking the half hour.

"Come on," she said. "We have to get this letter back to Mama, before she discovers it's gone. She means this to be a secret. We don't want her to know we read it. This whole thing has been hard enough on her. It'd break her heart if she thought we knew the real truth. You and your big idea."

"I only . . ." I started to say, but thought better of it.

Katherine looked at me with her schoolteacher look and pointed her finger at me. "Don't breathe a word of this to anyone."

She annoyed me when she got so bossy, but I knew what was best and we started to walk back together. We held hands and our bare feet made a flat, soft sound on the dry, caked ground. The ache in my stomach felt like a horse had kicked me right square in the belly button.

The letter in my apron pocket grew hotter and hotter with each step. The closer we got to the house, the more convinced I was that Papa's letter was going to burn a hole clean through my apron pocket.

I was never so sorry I stole something in all my life.

CHAPTER TWO

August 26, 1909

Katherine and I found Mama on the way back to the house. She was on the ground like a piece of firewood fallen out of a stack just waiting for a passerby to pick up.

"Quick. Go get help," Katherine cried out. She knelt down and grabbed Mama's arm. "Mama, wake up! Wake up!" she kept calling out. Katherine used her apron to fan Mama's face.

"Don't stand there gawking, Callie. Hurry!" Katherine ordered.

I started my knees pumping and ran as fast as I could for the house.

"Come quick! Come quick! It's Mama," I hollered as I went past the chicken house and scattered half a dozen of Mama's prized Rock Island Reds.

Opa hurried out the kitchen door. He rushed past me, his cane in his right hand and his straw hat with the black band in the other. The carcass of a freshly plucked chicken lay on the chopping block, feathers and a bucket of hot water on the ground. Aunt Mary was coming from the porch with a meat cleaver in her hand.

Thump . . . tap, thump . . . tap, thump . . . tap. Opa hurried down the path. I was his shadow. He stood over Mama for a split second, shading her body and shaking his head.

"Vorsicht! Vorsicht!" he ordered and pointed his cane at the house. Aunt Mary was right behind us, clucking her tongue, her hand covering her mouth. She rolled Mama over and felt the side of her neck for a pulse. Then Aunt Mary unfastened the top buttons of Mama's tight blouse.

"We've got to get her out of this sun and into the house," she told Opa. Arza and Algis came over from the barn looking almost as frightened and helpless as I felt. Aunt Mary motioned for them to lend a hand.

"Langsam!" Opa told them sharply. "Sachte, sachte!"

The two young men struggled with Mama's lifeless body. Her petticoats and skirts made picking her up very difficult.

"I'll carry her to the house," a deep voice boomed. We looked up to see Bert Goodner, the blacksmith. We were lucky he was smithing for us that day, fixing the busted axle on the hay wagon.

In one motion, he worked his giant, smoke-smudged arms underneath Mama, the muscles bulging as they went to work gently scooping her up. As easily as if Mama had been a doll, Bert lifted her off the ground. He went from kneeling to one knee. He stopped momentarily, then ever so gently, took one of his mammoth hands and carefully brushed off a spot on his chest. He turned Mama's head so it rested on his leather apron.

"Go get Mrs. Fancher," Aunt Mary told Arza. "We're gonna have a baby here before we planned on it."

While the others followed Aunt Mary into the house, Katherine pulled me aside.

"Look what we did to Mama," she said and started to cry. "I'm sure Mama was coming to find us. She was looking for her letter. I know that's what it was. She must've been fretting over it." Tears ran down Katherine's cheeks. "We did this to her. We got her upset, now she's gonna have the baby and it's too early. It's all our fault." Katherine leaned against the house.

"No, that's not true," I told her, only half-believing my own words. But Aunt Mary was calling us and there was no more time to talk it over.

"You girls stay out of the way, you hear?" Aunt Mary warned, her finger pointing at us. She could manage to point at both of us at the same time. "Stay close to the house," she told us, "in case I need you."

Katherine and I took the basket of old clothes Mama kept on the back porch and began cutting quilt squares. Our ears were pitched for the slightest noise from the house. The two of us sat in the shade listening and waiting as the clock struck the hours away. The rhythmic sound of Bert smithing in the barn was a comfort. The steady wham of his hammer pounding on metal and the light ting of his set stroke put a pulsing beat in the air. Wham, Ting. Wham, wham, Ting. Wham, Ting. Wham, wham, Ting.

We saw the buggy come clipping along with our neighbor, Mrs. Fancher, and Arza inside. Mrs. Fancher hurried into the house, not even stopping to say hello. Arza followed behind her with a big carpet bag.

"You're mixing them together, Callie," Katherine said crossly as I laid a green plaid square into a pile of red calico. But even Katherine had mislaid a square or two herself, since our minds weren't fully on our work. Only once did we hear something.

"Those are birthing pains," Katherine volunteered, suddenly acting like she knew everything there was in the world about having babies. "I remember from when I heard Mama have you. Mama said you came out upside down and backward," Katherine told me, sounding very pleased with herself.

"Oh really?" I answered. "And I suppose you came out perfect, huh? Wearing a little frilly bonnet and your best Sunday dress!" Maybe I didn't know much about how babies came out, but at least I knew they came out all naked.

A cry, almost a scream, caught us both by surprise. I watched as my hands started to shake.

"How long does it take to have a baby?" I whispered.

"Sometimes hours, sometimes days," Katherine answered, suddenly turning pale.

A stillness came over the house, the kind that comes up before a storm. As the clock struck six times, Algis and Arza walked over from the barn. Bert's hammering stopped. All of us were there on the porch watching and waiting, too frightened to say a word when Aunt Mary came to the back door.

"Your mother's asked to see you, girls," she said sternly, pointing her finger wildly at us. "Don't, you hear me, DON'T speak unless you're spoken to.

And if you do, don't say anything to upset your mother. Understand?"

"Yes, Aunt Mary," Katherine answered for both of us.

Algis and Arza followed us into the house.

We tagged along behind Aunt Mary, down the dark hallway and into Mama's bedroom. The door was ajar, but Aunt Mary pushed it all the way open. I caught my breath and grabbed Katherine's hand. We both saw the tiny bundle in Mama's arms at the same time. But the smell and the heat of the room stopped us at the doorway.

Something was terribly wrong. Two dark winter blankets had been put over the windows. There was hardly an extra breath of air in the room. The smell of camphor was everywhere. I remember taking in a chestful of the mediciny fumes and trying to stay steady on my feet.

Mrs. Fancher was standing at the head of Mama's big double bed, and Opa was sitting on a chair beside the night table, holding onto Mama's hand. He rested his forehead on the curved part of his cane and didn't even look at us when we came into the room.

Mama's eyes opened and looked so bright. Every face in the room was turned to watch her.

"Are the girls here, Mary?" she whispered.

"Yes, Elschen, they're here."

Aunt Mary pushed us closer.

"Katherine," Mama called out, "Katherine, are you there?"

Mama's eyes were open, but why wasn't she seeing us?

"Is she blind?" I whispered in Katherine's ear.

Aunt Mary shushed me, and Katherine shook her head.

"I'm here, Mama," Katherine answered obediently.

"And my Callie?"

"I'm here, Mama." I started to reach out to touch her, but Aunt Mary tapped the back of my hand.

"Oh, my sweet little girls," Mama sighed. "Come and see your new brother."

Mama raised her hand ever so slightly as she spoke, letting go of Opa's hand. As he looked at us, I saw tears running down his cheeks into his white beard.

"A lovely baby, such a big boy for your Papa." Mama put her hand on the bundle nestled in her arm. "Your father will be pleased." She sighed again. Her hand looked so pale against the white sheets.

Katherine and I watched, but there was no movement. No tiny cries.

Mama caressed the blankets again. This time a

corner fell back. That was when we saw the waxy, grayish face of our beautifully featured baby brother. A baby brother surely dead long before he was born on that hot August afternoon. His sweet hands clenched forever into tiny little fists.

I looked away from Mama and tried to get more air into my chest, since it suddenly felt like someone had hugged me too hard and too long around the ribs. When I looked down at the floor, I caught sight of a basin of bloody rags half-shoved under the bed. The room began to swirl before my eyes.

Everything was spinning. I squeezed Katherine's hand for all it was worth. Tears were welling up in my eyes. Faces became a blur. Katherine leaned across the bed and grabbed Mama's hand before it touched the dead infant again.

"Vati," Mama murmured, "ich bin so müde."

"Mama, we're right here. We're right here, it's your Katherine."

Katherine held onto Mama's hand. "It's Callie and me," she said. "You're gonna be fine, Mama."

"I want your papa to see his fine boy," Mama started to say, but her voice became less than a whisper.

"Algis," Aunt Mary said suddenly, "take the girls outside."

Before we turned away from the bed, we watched

Mrs. Fancher lean over Mama and shake her gently by the shoulders. We saw Mrs. Fancher feel the side of Mama's neck. Then Mrs. Fancher lifted Mama's wrist to feel a pulse.

"Quick," Mrs. Fancher said to Aunt Mary, "get me the mirror from the dresser."

Mrs. Fancher held the long-handled mirror right in front of Mama's mouth.

Two strong arms pulled us from behind and moved us toward the door. I looked over my shoulder as Mrs. Fancher turned to Opa.

"Lord help us, Johannes, I think she's gone," Mrs. Fancher said as though she could hardly believe it herself. "Elschen is dead."

"No!" Opa thundered. "No, that cannot be." He stood up, knocking the chair over. "She is the only thing I have!" he cried out. "Sie ist mein ein und alles. Oh mein Gott! Oh mein Gott!"

Poor Mrs. Fancher. She looked so frightened and bewildered.

"Elschen's gone, Mary," Mrs. Fancher said. She put her hands up to the sides of her face and started to sob. "I don't know what to do to bring her back."

Aunt Mary grabbed Mama's hand and patted it sharply as if the smack would make Mama wake up. Mama didn't move. Aunt Mary bent over to put her head on Mama's chest, listening for a heartbeat.

For a few brief seconds, there was silence in the

room. No one moved. No one uttered a word. Slowly, Aunt Mary stood upright. She looked from Opa to Mrs. Fancher, then back to Mama. The way Aunt Mary shook her head, I knew right then that our mama was dead.

CHAPTER THREE

Red Sky at Night

On toward evening, Mr. Fancher pulled up in the buggy with Harriet and Marie Louise. I was never so glad to see anyone. The four of us sat on the front porch, watching the sun set over the cornfields. The sky turned a brilliant reddish orange.

"Red sky at night, shepherd's delight," Marie Louise said as she stared out over the road and the field.

"Red sky at morning, shepherds take warning," Katherine finished. She and Marie Louise sat arm in arm. They were the best of friends and the very same age. They'd both graduated eighth grade in May and were going to be the teacher's assistants in the fall. Harriet and I shared a seat on the steps, the way we shared a desk in school. She gently rubbed my back. I had cried so hard I'd given myself the hiccups.

We watched another buggy turn into our lane.

Neighbors had been coming from all over to help. We could hear people inside the house already as they started the cleaning and baking for the next day's funeral.

"That beautiful sunset's for your mama," Harriet said. "I just know in my heart it is."

"Mama always loved a pretty sunset," Katherine said softly and started crying again. "She wasn't supposed to die," Katherine whispered. Marie Louise put an arm around Katherine's shoulder. From out on the porch, we could hear Opa, speaking in German to Uncle Mike.

"I want Papa," I said to Harriet, as though she could magically bring him back that very instant. "I want Papa to come home." And I started crying all over again, too.

"Look," Harriet said suddenly, "it's an auto-mobile," and she pointed toward Mule Barn Road.

A big shiny Model A chugged along the road and turned into our lane. We watched in amazement as it parked in the side yard, and a man in a black suit got out.

"Who's that?" I asked.

"That's Mr. Gulliford. He's the undertaker from Noblesville," Marie Louise answered.

"Why's he here?"

Katherine and Marie Louise looked at each other as though they didn't know what to say.

"Why's he here?" I asked again.

"He's come to make Mama look pretty for tomorrow," Katherine answered, and Marie Louise pulled out her own hankie.

Aunt Mary called us to come in the house. As we walked through the front hall, we saw the neighbor women dusting and shaking out curtains while the men were helping move furniture to make a place for the coffin in the parlor.

Dusk was settling on the steamy countryside as we began hauling buckets of water from the pump for our baths. Aunt Mary had placed a washtub in the kitchen. She'd strung up an old quilt across one corner for privacy. Katherine and I shared the tub. Aunt Mary stood on the other side of the curtain to make sure we scrubbed behind our ears and used the bar of lye soap on the bottoms of our feet.

"And don't forget to find your shoes and stockings," she told us. "You'll need them for tomorrow." We both groaned quietly because we hadn't worn shoes since the last day of school in May. Marie Louise and Harriet handed us our towels over the curtain, and we could hear Algis talking with Aunt Mary out on the porch.

"But it seems like a waste of water to take a bath tonight, Ma," he was saying. "We're gonna be sleeping out in the barn, anyway." Algis and Arza were twins and looked as alike as two peas in a pod. They were covered from head to toe in chaff and dust from cleaning out the silo for when the threshers would come through.

"That doesn't matter," Aunt Mary answered. "Get yourselves on in here before the water gets any colder."

Katherine and I, wrapped in old sheets ripped in half, were heading upstairs as Algis and Arza came into the kitchen. Harriet and Marie Louise waited for us in our bedroom.

"But couldn't we have clean water?" Algis asked.

"What's in there is good enough," Aunt Mary answered.

"But maybe the girls . . ." Algis started to say.

"What did you say?" Aunt Mary asked, not hearing him clearly.

"Well, maybe the girls . . . you know . . . well, maybe the girls peed in the water," he finally managed to get out.

"Peed in the water!" I said indignantly from the stairs, loud enough to be heard all the way out to the barn.

I trooped down the steps, holding the wads of sheet around me.

"Listen to me, Algis Kreuzer, you want to take a bath in pee water? Well, I'll step right back in that tub and oblige you." I hardly got the last words out before Katherine was hauling me up the steps by a handful of sheet.

"Who does he think he is?" I muttered, pulling my nightgown over my head.

Katherine was putting hers on, too. I watched the nightie drift down around her ankles. Even in her old hand-me-downs, Katherine looked lovely. She sat on the edge of the bed, and Marie Louise took the hairbrush from the top of the dresser.

"This is the loveliest red hair I ever saw," she told Katherine. That's what I thought, too. Katherine's auburn hair had dried into wispy curls around her face, and her milky-colored skin was dotted with peach-colored freckles.

And me, well, I always thought I had the looks of a frog. Kind of short and spindly legs, bug eyes, and hair the color of mud. I wasn't a thing like Katherine or Mama.

"Ribbitt," I said quietly. Harriet looked at me and laughed. "She looks like a princess and I look like a frog," I told Harriet. "Frog's fur, that's what my hair looks like. Frog's fur!"

Katherine gave me a cross look. Harriet took two handfuls of my thick curls and held them up like pig's ears. She used a comb and worked at my hair for a little while, but it was nearly hopeless, the curls were snarled and tangled.

Harriet and Marie Louise left not long after that. Katherine and I sat at the end of the bed and waved to them from the window. "We'll see you tomorrow," Harriet called, before they passed through the gate.

"At Mama's funeral," Katherine finished somberly. She crawled under the covers, and I lit the lamp and began scouting around the room. I patrolled for bedbugs and when I found one, I knocked it off into the glass hurricane lamp, happy to see it fall into the flame and sizzle. Mama usually did the bedbug patrol every night before she tucked us in. I blew out the flame and crawled into bed next to Katherine.

We lay there with the window wide open and a band of moonlight falling across the covers.

We didn't say anything for a long time. People were leaving in their buggies, and we heard the last one finally pull away. Even the Model A was gone. The house was quiet again and we heard the thud of the clasp on the barn door as Arza closed it from the inside.

"Did we kill Mama?" Katherine asked.

"I don't think we did," I told her honestly, not really knowing if what I said was absolutely true or not. "Mrs. Fancher said Mama lost too much blood. I know we didn't make her do that." I bit my lip so I wouldn't start to cry. "Besides, the baby was dead

a long time before it was born. Mrs. Fancher told
me."

We lay there in the darkness and held hands.

"Did you see the baby, too?" Katherine asked.

"Yes," I answered quietly. "He was beautiful. His
tiny little nose was like a button, and his cheeks
were so round." I'd been looking forward to a little
brother or sister for months. I loved babies so. I
told everyone I knew how I wanted to have a whole
houseful of children when I grew up.

"What's gonna happen to us, Callie?" Katherine
asked. She gave a long sniff and wiped her eyes
with the sleeve of her nightie.

"I don't know," I told her. "I don't even think
Papa can come home. He said he had nothing left
after that man swindled him out of his money." I
reached under my pillow for the hankie I'd hidden
there and dabbed my runny nose.

"I'm so scared," I told Katherine.

"I wish Papa would hurry and come home," she
said softly.

We lay in the darkness and eventually heard the
clock strike twelve times. Katherine's breathing
grew slow and steady, and I knew she was asleep. I
could hear Opa shuffling around downstairs.

I slipped out of bed, hoping maybe I could sit
with him for a while. I started down the stairs, but

I saw him take his Bible from the table and sit down to write.

I knew there were names in Opa's Bible. Family names. A whole long page of them written in his curly, old-world handwriting. Bits of lace in there, too. Locks of baby's hair with ribbons tied round the curls and newspaper clippings.

There was a small piece of newsprint about Uncle Erich. The obituary told how he'd died young of trichinosis, only being over in the United States for a few years and leaving Aunt Mary to raise Arza and Algis all on her own. And the clipping about Oma, Opa's wife, and how she'd died in childbirth having our mother. Opa's Bible seemed like a sorrowful book to me. Recounting the sad things in life. The "comings and goings of life" was what Mama always called it. The births and deaths and marriages and christenings. The very first entry was when Opa came to America. There beside his name, it read; Johannes Günther Kreuzer to America—1861.

As a young man, my grandfather had shocked more fields of wheat and hauled more loads of hay than most young men ever did in a lifetime to earn his passage to America. Within five years he'd saved the money to buy tickets for Michael and Erich. Together, the three of them planned and worked for farms of their own. Farmland out West. That's what the newspapers had talked of. But their money had run out as far west as Indiana and the three men had settled in Bakers Corner. Uncle Michael never married. Uncle Erich died at twenty-seven, leaving Aunt Mary a bitter widow with a run-down boardinghouse and twin babies to raise. After only a year of marriage, Opa was a widower. We had heard the story many times about how he raised Mama all by himself.

From between the stair railings, I watched Opa write in his Bible. The comings and goings of other people's lives had suddenly become the comings and goings in my life. I knew Opa was looking for my mother's name. Her little piece of history. El-schen Marie Kreuzer Common. As Opa dipped his pen into the ink bottle, I wanted to cry out, "Don't write that date, Opa."

His putting August 26, 1909, after her name meant that she was gone. It made her passing very real. And if there was one thing I didn't want to be real, it was Mama's death.

I heard the scratching of Opa's pen from across the room. I watched as he mopped the tears on his cheeks with his handkerchief. I felt so numb inside that I wondered how my feet could find the steps underneath them as I climbed back upstairs. I crawled into bed next to Katherine. Even though she was asleep, I tried to hold her hand. I lay there in the dark, listening to her steady breathing. I put my hand over my chest and felt my heart beating and beating. Pum-pum. Pum-pum. Pum-pum. I wondered why my heart was still going and Mama's had stopped. I blinked away the tears, and they dripped down into my ears.

Every time I closed my eyes I could see Mama's face and hear her voice as clear as a bell. "Oh, my sweet little girls," she'd called us. I remembered how she'd tried to hug me that very morning and give me a kiss. But I was in such a hurry that the kiss had brushed past my cheek and landed somewhere near my ear. I thought for sure I could still feel the touch of her lips on my face. I put my hand up to my temple to try and find the spot. I wanted to keep the feel of Mama's kiss from never fading away, and that was how I fell asleep the night my mama died.

CHAPTER FOUR

Mama's Funeral

The sun was high in the sky, and the cicadas were already screeching their song to the August heat by the time we woke up the next morning. My head pounded. My eyes felt swollen and puffy. They stung each time I rubbed them.

Katherine and I pulled our best Sunday dresses out of the trunk by the foot of the bed.

"Mothballs have a powerful smell, don't they?" I said, handing her the caramel-colored dress Mama had made out of old curtains. Katherine's hair nearly matched the satiny color. Mama had crocheted cream-colored bands of lace for the collar and sleeves.

"Open it up again," Katherine ordered. I sighed since I knew she'd remembered Aunt Mary's orders about the stockings.

"But they're so hot and itchy, Katherine."

"Aunt Mary said . . ." Katherine started to say.

"All right, I can hear you," I answered. Two pairs of miserably thick, wool stockings waited for me, tucked into one of the pockets in the lid of the trunk. I could feel the itch already as I held them in my sweaty hand.

"Ugh," I said. We both knew Mama's rule.

"Stockings go on November first and stay on until May Day," she'd say in October. And by the end of April, we'd be itching and scratching. Then we'd get a lecture from Mama.

"It's not ladylike to scratch in public!" Mama would whisper.

While Katherine brushed her hair and fixed a ribbon in the back, I put on my faded blue dress. Every single button was tight all the way down the front, and I had to leave the collar buttons open. Katherine and I had both grown considerably over the summer.

The bodice of Katherine's dress was plain. There was no room across the chest to accommodate the two bumps that seemed to be springing up.

"You're getting b-o-s-o-m-s," I spelled. I pointed at her and giggled.

"Oh, Callie," she said, exasperated. "Mama says I'm becoming a woman." She smacked my finger in annoyance.

I turned to face the wall. As Katherine put on her stockings, I stuffed mine into the front of my dress.

I turned around and waited quietly for her to look up. When she did, she laughed and said, "Careful there, one of your bosoms is crawling out of your dress." She pointed to the sock dangling between two of my buttons. I could barely squeeze my feet into my high-button shoes and no matter how hard I tried, I could only get half the buttons to hook.

Katherine and I stood at the top of the stairs for a long time before we could bring ourselves to go down them. From the first few steps, we could see the edge of Mama's coffin.

"I think my heart's gonna pound right out of my chest," I whispered to Katherine.

"Mine, too," she said softly. She started to cry and took out a hankie she had tucked into the sleeve of her dress.

We stood next to each other by Mama's coffin, Katherine and I, our arms wrapped around each other. I hurt so much inside I couldn't speak. Even breathing seemed to make the ache in my chest go deeper and deeper.

We watched Aunt Mary arrange the edge of one of Mama's favorite blue quilts over the sides of the coffin. Aunt Mary smoothed Mama's hair back and fussed with her lace collar and buttons. Aunt Mary tenderly patted Mama on the shoulder. The tiny bundle of our brother lay tucked in alongside Mama's right arm.

"I feel so bad about the baby," Katherine said.

"We didn't even get to name him," I told her. "We could have called him Walter. Walter is such a fine name." I was crying hard and could barely get the words out. I nestled my face deeper into her shoulder and tear spots moistened the material.

Two buggies pulled into the yard. Aunt Mary stepped back and straightened up. She smoothed her apron and tucked stray wisps of hair back into place.

"Pull yourself together, Callie. People are here to pay their respects to your mother," Aunt Mary ordered. I mopped my wet cheeks with a hankie and gave a long sniff.

Aunt Mary stepped outside the parlor door to greet the first of the funeral callers.

"Wait a minute," I heard Katherine say. She quickly went back up the stairs to our room. I stood near the coffin and looked at Mama. She barely looked like Mama to me. She looked so stiff. I wanted to touch her. I wanted her to wake up. When I stepped closer to look at her face, I gasped and felt myself get dizzy. There were tiny stitch marks along her lips to keep her mouth closed. I was holding onto the coffin with one hand to steady myself when Katherine came down the stairs.

She tiptoed across the room.

"This should be buried with Mama," she whispered, holding up Papa's letter. "It's the last thing she had from him."

"But . . ." was the only word I managed to get out as Katherine leaned over the side of the coffin. First, she reached for Mama's mottled hands, then hesitated, before moving toward the bundle of our baby brother.

"Shouldn't you . . ." I started to say.

But Katherine had a determined look on her face.

"Wouldn't it . . . ?" I whispered, watching Katherine extend her arm.

In one swift motion, Katherine grabbed hold of Mama's folded hands, the letter poised to slide under them. But Katherine quickly let go.

"Oh dear God," she cried and drew back in horror.

I hurried around to the other side of the coffin and put my arm around Katherine's shoulders. I took the letter from her and hid it in one of the folds of the quilt.

"Mama's as cold as ice," Katherine gasped.

"Didn't you know?" I asked. "Opa stayed through the night with Mama in the springhouse."

Katherine shook her head as I helped her walk over to the stairs. She was trembling and shaking.

She sat down, and I put my arm around her. She was shivering over and over again even with the heat. She kept staring at the coffin and rubbing her dress with the hand that had touched Mama.

Another wagonload of neighbors pulled into the yard as Aunt Mary and Mrs. Achleitner came into the room. They both stared at Mama.

"You've done a nice job, Mary," Mrs. Achleitner said, standing with her purse dangling on her arm and practically leaning into Mama's coffin. "Elschen looks peaceful for sure. It's a good sign when the body has a peaceful look to it. Sometimes they don't, you know. Their faces are all twisted and full of pain."

Mrs. Achleitner fanned herself with her hand, then pointed toward Mama.

"She's turned blotchy, of course, but that can't be helped with this heat. Why, I saw a body laid out once over at a family's house on the Boxley Road . . ."

"Girls," Aunt Mary said rather loudly. We both stood up. "We'll be starting soon."

"I tell you, Mary Kreuzer, you people have had more than your share of bad times. Now Elschen dying in childbirth. And Owen gone off to who-knows-where in Oregon. Why I wonder what's gonna become of these girls. I do, I do."

"We'll stay here with Opa until our papa . . ." I

started to say, but Katherine gave my hand a hard squeeze. I looked at Aunt Mary. She was standing as stiff as a fence post and grinding her false teeth together. She had that look whenever someone was testing her patience and I was glad, for once, I wasn't the one.

The side door opened, and people started quietly milling into the room. There must've been twenty people crowded into our parlor that sweltering August morning. Uncle Mike and Opa came in together. Opa leaned heavily upon his cane. Opa, Katherine, and I sat in chairs right in front of the coffin. Mrs. Fancher had picked a bucketful of gladiolas and hollyhocks and set them at the foot of the pine box. People sat on the only other chairs we had, and when these were used up, they stood with hats and bonnets in their hands.

Pastor Greene from the Friends' Church began the sermon as soon as the clock finished striking eleven.

"Let us bow our heads in prayer. Oh Lord," he said loudly, in his preacher's voice, "we beseech thee . . ."

I know they read from Proverbs, chapter thirty-one, verse ten, but I only caught bits and pieces of the sermon. I pulled at the collar of my dress, and the buttons tugged across my tummy. The itching behind my knees felt like a thousand fire ant bites.

I kept an eagle eye on Katherine, too. She looked so pale and her hands were clammy and cold. I could see sweat dripping down the sides of her face. My own upper lip tasted salty.

At one point Opa stood up and read in German from his Bible. He was standing without his cane and I could see his knees shaking underneath his pants. "Zweiter Timotheus," he said in a crackly voice. "Denn ich werde schon goepfert und die Zeit meines Abscheidens ist vorhanden . . ." At the end of the passage, he stopped reading. He dabbed at his eyes with his hankie and sang so very softly, "Schlaf, Kindchen, schlaf."

"Sleep, little one, sleep," I murmured, remembering the many nights Mama had sung the same lullaby to Katherine and me at bedtime. The tears welled up in my eyes and spilled down my cheeks. Uncle Mike helped Opa sit down.

Quietly, he said to Pastor Greene, "Up it must close."

Aunt Mary motioned for Katherine and me to stand. "It's time to kiss your Mama good-bye," she commanded. Katherine was crying hard. She leaned over and kissed Mama on the cheek. When it was my turn, I slowly bent over the edge of the coffin.

I meant to kiss Mama like I was supposed to. Oh, I wanted to kiss her. I wanted to do like I was told.

But Mama looked so cold. Her skin was so mottled. She had such a stern look to her. I put my head close to hers, but truth to tell is, my lips never touched her cheek.

Bert Goodner and two other men brought the lid of the coffin forward and Aunt Mary began pulling the edges of the quilt up and over Mama. Aunt Mary took off Mama's wedding ring.

"This belongs to you now, Katherine." Aunt Mary handed her the thin, gold band. Katherine's hand held mine tighter and tighter as Aunt Mary moved around the coffin, laying the folds of the quilt over Mama. Aunt Mary reached across to pull up one last corner. She gave a tug. The letter flipped into the air. Katherine cried out. I felt Katherine's hand let go of mine.

Everyone in the room gasped. Katherine had collapsed in a heap on the floor. Several people clustered around Katherine and started fanning her while I carefully and quietly picked up the letter and tucked it into the top of my high-button shoe.

CHAPTER FIVE

Orion's Belt

After everyone returned from the cemetery, Katherine wanted to rest. On my way back upstairs from refilling the water pitcher for her, I heard voices coming from the kitchen. I stopped in the hallway, nearly out of sight and stood by the hat rack. The water pitcher grew heavier and heavier by the second. I hugged the slippery pitcher to my stomach with both arms.

"Whatever's gonna become of those girls, Mary?" I heard one of the voices ask.

"It'll be a long cold day in July before Owen Common shows his face here again in Bakers Corner," another voice said.

"A man doesn't steal money from his own flesh and blood and then waltz back to take up where he left off, unless he's a fool. He'd be better off starting a new life for himself out West. His relatives are nothing but a bunch of drifters anyway."

"Wouldn't surprise me if he never showed up again."

"Don't be so hard on him, Isabelle. I heard tell it was only five hundred dollars that he stole."

"Five hundred! It was more like fifteen hundred."

I nearly gave myself away as I started to say, "My papa's gonna come back for us," but I remembered in the nick of time. My arms were beginning to ache. The pitcher felt like it was as heavy as a basket of rocks, so I set it down on the floor by my feet.

"Doesn't matter how much it was," Aunt Mary said. I could tell by the way she was talking that she was clicking her false teeth together between words. "Why, Johannes and the girls, they've got nothing now. Johannes never did have enough money to buy this farm, and old man Palmgren only leases it to Johannes every year out of the goodness of his heart."

"Whatever's gonna become of them?" I recognized the voice as Mrs. Fancher's.

"There's a teaching post open in District Number Twelve," someone suggested. "Katherine's good with the young ones. She could make fifteen or eighteen dollars a month teaching school."

"What a waste of her time," Aunt Mary answered.

"Katherine could work for me at the boarding-house. I could use a cook." Aunt Mary made it sound as though the discussion was ended. I heard the screen door squeak open and nothing was said for a few seconds. When I peeked around the corner, I saw Opa standing by the door with his hat in his hands.

"What is this about my Katerina," he said with authority. "Somewhere she is going?" He was squinting his eyes and staring at Aunt Mary.

"Katherine's going to work at the boardinghouse for me in Westfield. There ought to be one person in your family bringing in a little money."

Opa threw his hat down on the table. The women in the room stared at the straw brim scooting across the oilcloth. Opa's face was getting red and his hands shook as he reached for the table to steady himself.

"Maybe I say where Katherine goes," he said firmly.

"Have you counted the change in your pocket recently, Johannes?" Aunt Mary replied.

I heard a gasp and there was a nervous stirring in the room. People seemed to be trying to gather things together to leave. Two or three people coughed. I tried my hardest to melt back into the wall.

"You are speaking out of turn, Mary," I heard Opa say.

"Oh, is that so," Aunt Mary replied. "And just how do you propose to pay the undertaker for Elschen's funeral?"

"Mary," Mrs. Fancher said quickly, "Elschen's only been in the grave a few hours. Shouldn't this wait?"

"That undertaker's gonna want fifteen dollars by the end of the month, Johannes. Fifteen for the funeral and another thirty for the cemetery plot. Believe me, I remember what it was like when Erich died." I heard the sharp click, click, click of Aunt Mary's heels on the kitchen floor. "You got an extra fifteen dollars?"

There was a long pause and as he said, "Nein," very softly, I felt my heart skip a beat.

"Katherine's not like Callie," I heard Aunt Mary say. "Katherine's a good, hard worker." My face suddenly flushed with anger.

"Katherine'll make good money. She can live in the room off the attic."

There was a long silent pause, and everyone in the kitchen stopped moving around as they waited for Opa's answer.

"A fine teacher Katherine would make," I heard Opa say as I picked up the water pitcher. "A fine teacher."

"She'll make more money cooking for me at the boardinghouse. Might even meet a decent man and get married. Then she'd be off your hands for good."

"Nein," he answered quickly. "My girls are good girls. They cause no problems. I don't want them married off. It is better Katherine becomes a teacher. To use her brain is the highest kind of work. She has a good, strong mind."

"Well, you can think your highfalutin thoughts if you want. If she doesn't get that teaching job, why she can come work for me."

"I take good care of my family," Opa said quietly. "Just you see, Mary Kreuzer."

"It's not that, Johannes," Aunt Mary replied. "You'll be down to your last dollar in a few weeks, and Katherine's old enough now to bring in what money she can for the family."

"We get by," I heard Opa say. "This schoolteacher's job? It begins in a few weeks, ja?"

"Yes," Aunt Mary answered. "But Katherine could come and cook for me at the boardinghouse until then."

"No," was on my lips, but as I turned to say it, I whammed the side of the pitcher into the doorframe. There was a crash and a splash. The milky-white pitcher smashed into a million pieces, spilling water all over the floor. Shards of porcelain scattered into the kitchen. The only thing left in my hand was the handle.

"Oh, for mercy's sake," was the first thing Aunt Mary said. "Little pitchers have big ears, don't you know, Callie?" she moaned. "You're always into no good. You take after your father, don't you? The nut doesn't fall far from the tree, does it, Callie?"

"My papa's not . . ." I started to say.

"Enough," Opa said. "Genug."

"Don't you worry, honey," said Mrs. Fancher as she put her arm around me and helped me step over the chips of porcelain on the floor.

"It's not the first pitcher that's been broke and it won't be the last. Don't you let it worry you none," she said quietly, picking up the bits and pieces and putting them into our aprons. As we knelt down, I saw Opa take out the little vial of heart pills from his vest pocket. I knew he would put one under his tongue.

Along about dusk, the last wagon turned out of our lane. As the stars were coming out, Opa went to sit on the front porch and have a smoke. I tagged along behind him. He tamped tobacco into the bowl of his pipe and the flame from the match he held across the bowl was sucked in. He blew two or three puffs of smoke before blowing the last cloud into a ring. I tried to poke my finger through the middle.

Katherine came out on the porch, too. The three

of us didn't really say much. We stared toward the end of the lane. Some distance away, we saw three deer cross the road; a doe, a fawn, and a buck.

"What's gonna happen now, Opa?" Katherine asked. She had pulled one of Mama's old, lacy shawls around her shoulders. A light mist hung over the countryside about waist high. When I was little, I'd run out into the fields and try to catch it with my hands. That mist was always just out of reach.

"A little I've been thinking on this," Opa replied quietly. He took a few more puffs on his pipe.

"I keep thinkin' Mama's gonna step right out here on the porch with us any minute," I said softly. "It doesn't seem real to me that she's gone."

Opa put his arm around me. "It is your heart that wants to see her, Herzchen. Es braucht Zeit. It takes time. It will take much time for you to understand. A long time for each one of us to understand that she is gone."

"How soon till I have to go and interview for the teaching job, Opa?" Katherine asked.

"I figure we have two, maybe three weeks."

"That quickly?" she replied.

"Oh no, I don't want you to go. I wish they needed a teacher here at Bakers Corner," I told Katherine.

"Ja, so soon and so far away, it is." Opa put his

other arm around Katherine. "Much I have been thinking on this. I do not want it this way, but I cannot think us another answer." He ran his fingers through his white hair.

"An old man like me. They don't want. Sit down here, old-timer, they always say," and he motioned toward the steps. "I'm strong and healthy for my seventy-five years. Ahhh," he sighed, "it is awful when you get old and no one has a use for you."

"But you still have us, Opa. You can take care of me," I offered.

Opa's eyes brightened in the growing darkness. "Ja, mein Schatz." He ruffled my hair. "We have each other. Und in der Zwischenzeit, there is work, work, work."

"The threshers will be coming through anytime now," Katherine said.

"And there's the kraut to put up," I added, sticking out my tongue and making a puckered-up face.

"And sorghum to cut. A lot we have to do. All this will help."

"Yes, and it will help us get more money," I said thoughtfully.

"And I can send you my money from teaching. I'm old enough to work," Katherine said proudly.

"Ja, mein Liebchen, this is quite true. But it will

help our hearts more," he answered, looking up at the night sky.

"I wish with all my heart I didn't have to leave," Katherine said.

"Me, too," I chimed in.

"Up there," Opa said, pointing toward the sky. "Do you see those blinking, winking stars?" Opa looked at Katherine and me. "When I was a young man in the old country, we used to say the stars were people in heaven. Whenever the stars were sparkling and twinkling, it meant that the people in heaven were saying hello."

"Maybe Mama is talking to us right this very moment," I said.

"Of course she is," Katherine replied.

"And can you find Orion's Belt?" He held his hand so I could look right off the end of his index finger. That's when I spotted it. The three stars in a row.

"There it is," Katherine answered, after Opa helped her for a minute.

"Close your eyes," he commanded. "Now open them again and find it on your own. Teach yourself to find Orion's Belt. Always in the sky, it is. And brightest in the winter months to come. Do you see the three of us up there?" Opa whispered.

I looked at Opa for a minute.

"We're right here on the porch, Opa!" I laughed.

"Ja, Miss Smarty Pants, that is true. But once again, look." And he pointed toward the sky, in the direction of Orion's Belt. "Katherine, you see," and he pointed to the top star. "She is there. I am in between you. Ja, und mein Herzchen, you are next to me. Now do you see us?" he asked. "A secret place in the heart for us. Always we are there, the three of us. Sitting the way we are now. And if we should be separated, we have only to look up to the sky to see each other, ja?"

"Always together, Opa," I said, nestling my head into his vest. I could smell the scent of pipe tobacco and feel the scratch of wool against my cheek.

"The first night I'm gone, I can look up at the sky for you," Katherine said.

"Ja, meine Katerina, I am proud of you to be a teacher. And your mama, so proud she would be," he said.

"Just think, Opa. I'll have a real job. My first work for pay."

"Ja, each of us will have work. Callie and me our work here. And you to be a schoolteacher." Opa set his pipe down and put his arms around each of us. "We have our jobs," he said, his voice cracking, "but our hardest work is yet ahead of us."

"What's that?" I asked, looking at him.

"Für uns geht das Leben weiter ohne eure Mutti," he said slowly and tears rolled down into his beard. "Life goes on without your mother."

Opa held us very tightly. "And to go on living without your mother will be the hardest work of all." Katherine and I put our arms around him and we hugged and hugged.

CHAPTER SIX

The Threshing Dinner

"Has Opa written to Papa?" I asked Katherine for the hundredth time the morning the threshing crews were due to arrive.

"I'm sure Opa did," she replied.

"Then why hasn't Papa come home yet?"

"Callie, you've asked me that a million times and if I've told you once, I've told you a dozen times. Letters take at least two weeks to get out West. And it's only been two weeks since Mama died." Katherine was plucking feathers off a big pullet. A pan of scalding water was on a tree stump. Katherine ker-plopped the bird into the water one more time. "I'm sure Papa will get back here as soon as he can."

"I heard Mrs. Achleitner say Papa'd be a fool to show his face here again, seeing as how everyone knows he stole the money from Opa."

"Don't be dumb, Callie," Katherine answered with her hand on her hip. She wiped a lock of hair out of her face with her forearm and bent over the chicken again, pulling off a handful of feathers. "Papa wouldn't forget about us. Besides, what you heard was idle gossip."

"Are we really poor?" I asked.

"I don't actually know," she answered. "But I do know that I'll be able to make some money teaching. That ought to get us through the winter along with whatever we can get from selling the corn and wheat."

Two horse teams pulled into the yard while I was out by the clothesline taking down bags of drying cheese curds. I waved at the drivers, remembering them from last year. The teams were the same beautifully matched chestnuts with ink-black manes and tails. The driver of the loader waved first, then the driver of the thresher followed. The wheat, already cut and bundled into shocks, had been left to dry in the fields. On threshing day, the sheaves of wheat were brought over to the barn and thrown with pitchforks into the huge threshing machine. The grain was then separated from the straw. The straw, blown off into a large heap, created a natural slide for the children to play on. Once, I even saw Mama take a turn sliding down the straw stack. Bags of the newly harvested grain were taken to the granary to be sold. As the loader headed toward the forty acres beyond the stream, I heard the driver call out to the lead horse, "Haw, Gertie, haw." The team moved with precision and made a sharp turn to the left.

Back then, farms were buzzing with activity at threshing time. Men worked in the fields or made sure equipment was in running order while the women kept the field-workers fed from sunup to sundown. Neighbors came from farms all around to help in the house and out in the fields. Eight women were crowded into our small farmhouse kitchen cooking for the threshers that day. I had never seen so many ladies helping at threshing time, but then we had never been without a woman living in our house.

"A little more cream on this," Harriet told me as we stirred and salted and added a pinch of sugar to the big bowls of cottage cheese we were making. All my favorite aromas were coming out of our kitchen that day. They floated around the parlor air—the smells of biscuits and breads, beef drippings turning into gravy and tureens filled with chunks of chicken meat and squares of dumplings. The pungent smells of seven sweets and seven sours tickled my nose with corn chowchows and relishes. The curls and twists of cinnamon and nutmeg in persimmon or date puddings and sugar cream pies landed squarely in my very empty stomach.

Mrs. Fancher stood at the stove frying chicken, while Marie Louise was next to her mother, stirring gravy.

"Is Bert gonna be here today?" someone asked Marie Louise.

"Don't know," she answered with a blush, "but it would be nice, wouldn't it?"

"He's certainly the most eligible man in the county," one of the other women added.

"He'd make a fine husband."

As Katherine stepped up to the stove, one of the women pulled the hair off her shoulders and loosely braided it down her back.

"That's the loveliest head of hair I've seen in a long time, Katherine Common," she said, tying a piece of string in a bow at the end of the braid.

"Thank you," Katherine answered politely. She pushed up her sleeves and pulled out a straw from the broom. She opened the oven door and held the straw in the middle of the oven, counting "one one-thousand, two one-thousand, three one-thousand," until a small flame shot off the end of the straw. "Just right for the biscuits," she said. She dropped two short logs into the side firebox on the stove. A fire needed to be good and hot for baking biscuits properly.

Harriet and I covered our bowls of cottage cheese and carried them out to the back porch and stored them in a cool box filled with shaved ice. The box was barely big enough to hold the butter and cream, the bowls of cottage cheese, a platter of deviled eggs, and a dessert dish of tapioca pudding.

We skedaddled down the steps as fast as we could to a spot under the linden tree, where we had set out our dolls for a tea party. Although Mama had made us rag dolls, Papa thought our Lumpenpuppen were too plain and brought home store-bought dolls one day. Katherine and I kept them as clean and as new as the very first day they'd come out of their wrapping paper. Harriet's family was more worldly than ours and had many things we did not. She had her doll, Rose, long before I did. I had named my doll Victoria Isabella after two queens. We had our tea party using leaves as plates and tiny twigs as pretend spoons. We drank cool water from the pump and savored morsels of leftover pound cake in the midmorning heat. Later, we would share our spot with the women as they worked on a quilt Mama had nearly finished. Opa and his friend from the old country, Herr Baumeister, would play checkers there, too, in the shade and sweet fragrance of the tulip tree.

The men stopped work a little past noon and headed toward the side yard, where Harriet and I had set out two washtubs full of water and hung towels from the limbs of trees. The women put out fresh water from the pump for drinking, hanging the dipper off the side by a crook in the handle. The men rolled up their sleeves, if they hadn't already, and dipped their hands into the water, splashing the coolness all over their faces and up to their elbows. They used the big, square bars of lye soap we'd set out for them earlier.

The men found their places along the narrow dinner table under a shady spot of our linden tree by the kitchen door. Opa offered the grace before the meal.

"Gott im Himmel," he began loudly.

With my head bowed, I counted two platters of beef brisket on the table, a bowl of succotash, two bowls of piping hot green beans with slabs of bacon for flavoring, a crock of baked beans from scratch, a plate of hot cabbage salad, a basketful of Katherine's biscuits, a loaf each of dark and light rye bread, a bowl of mountainous mashed potatoes and two tureens of chicken and dumplings.

"I'm sure hoping Orpha Fancher made some of her fried chicken again," announced the man who ran the threshing machine. "It's the only reason I come up to this part of the state!"

I looked toward the kitchen door. Mrs. Fancher smiled as she stepped off the porch and came over to the table with a skillet heaped full of crispy fried chicken pieces.

"Maybe so, but I'm here for one of Marie Louise's lemon pies," another man said.

"Just pass me the biscuits," Bert said quietly, grinning up at Katherine.

Harriet and I were in charge of keeping the flies away. We used long branches from the peach tree, and we waved them over the table while the men ate. Marie Louise and Katherine walked around with pitchers of fresh-squeezed lemonade. All the other eligible girls kept offering Bert baked beans and dumplings or whatever hadn't been passed recently. By the time desserts were being served, Bert had so many plates of pie and cake in front of him, all he could do was laugh.

"Viele Hunde sind des Hasen Tod," Herr Baumeister said under his breath to Opa.

"What's that about a dog?" one of the men asked, recognizing a few words of German.

"With so many dogs, the rabbit has no chance," Opa translated, and everyone laughed again, even Bert.

If our farm had been the last one on the threshing ring, the men would've taken time to have a smoke and sit under the shade of the tulip tree in the yard, but there was still too much work ahead of them. They had horses to tend and machinery to check before traveling to the next farm. As they went back to the fields, they stopped by the kitchen door, tipped their hats, and paid their respects to all of the cooks.

"Mighty fine meal, ladies," a few of them said.

"I'll be back for your fried chicken again next year," the man working the threshing machine told Mrs. Fancher.

Around two o'clock, we set three buckets of switchel in the back of the wagon and took them out to the fields for the men to wet their whistles. It was said to quench a thirst faster than water. I never cared for the combination of lemonade, molasses and tea mixed together with a splash of vinegar.

By early evening, the neighbor women had nearly finished one of Mama's quilts. They'd put edging all around the border and had finished the white-thread pattern over the top of the basket-of-eggs design. The horses pulled the thresher through the yard once more and the men in charge of the steam engine greased up all the moving parts before it was taken to the next farm. I knew everyone would begin leaving soon, and I hated to see them go.

Harriet and I were gathering together our doll things when I heard Bert Goodner's deep voice behind me. I tuned my ears into the conversation even though I knew it wasn't polite to eavesdrop.

Bert Goodner stood stiffly in front of Opa, nearly squeezing the dickens out of the hat he held in both hands.

"Mr. Kreuzer. Sir," he said and cleared his throat.

"Ja, Bert," Opa replied, glancing up from his game of checkers.

"Mr. Kreuzer, I know this may not be the proper time and all, but I'm gonna ask anyway. Seein' as how Katherine's father is away, well, I thought I oughta ask you."

"Ja, Bert," Opa answered, puzzled. Bert had been blacksmithing for us ever since I could remember. "What is it, Bert? Did I forget to pay you?"

"No sir, Mr. Kreuzer," Bert started. "It's just that you, being Katherine's grandfather and all, well, I figure I should ask you now." He hesitated and looked down at the ground for a second. He had twisted his hat into a rumpled, felt ball. "Mr. Kreuzer," he began all over again, "I'd like to know if I can have your permission to come calling on Katherine."

"Oh," Opa replied at first. "A little I am going to have to think on this," he answered.

But I didn't have to think on it for a moment. I bounded out from underneath the tree like a jackrabbit and ran straight for the house.

"Katherine, Katherine," I called as I pulled open the back door so hard it whacked against the wall. "Katherine," I called, nearly out of breath. She was sitting at the quilting frame with all the other women, and I dove underneath it to come up right beside her.

"Guess what?" I said without waiting for an answer. "Bert Goodner wants to come calling on YOU!"

CHAPTER SEVEN

Spooning and Sparking

"What are you going to do if he tries to kiss you?" I asked Katherine the following Sunday evening. "Do you think he's going to try to hold your hand?"

"Oh, Callie," Katherine answered. She was fixing her hair into a long braid and putting in two tortoiseshell combs that had belonged to Mama. "He may not even come calling tonight. Opa didn't really know what to say, so he didn't exactly give Bert an answer."

"Do you think he's gonna ask you to marry him?"

"For heaven's sake, Callie, take it slower. First of all, I'm only fifteen and a half. Besides, the way it works is for a suitor to come calling. If he's a gentleman, he'll ask me on a buggy ride or two. Maybe we'll go to an ice-cream social at the church. We'll ride around in the buggy for a while, watch the stars, then maybe we'll hold hands. And maybe after a fashion, we might even do a little spooning."

"You mean kissing, don't you?"

"Oh, Callie, don't you know anything? Spooning is cuddling. And sparking," Katherine flushed a little, "well, that's the kissing part."

"Okay, then maybe you'll do a little sparking?"

"Not for a long time," she said sternly. "I suppose we'll have a few Sunday dinners with his folks. You know, things like that. We have to get to know each other first." She was beginning to sound really exasperated. "Marriage is a long way down the road, and you're getting the cart before the horse, Callie."

I climbed the stairs to a little flight of steps up to the attic. I looked out the window one more time. A tiny speck, the size of a collar button, was moving along Mule Barn Road. I looked away. I made myself slowly count from one to ten, then I looked again, and sure enough, the speck was getting bigger.

"He's coming! He's coming!" I shouted all the way down both sets of stairs until I found Opa and Katherine in the parlor.

"Oh, Callie, please be quiet. You're going to embarrass me. And you're making me nervous."

Opa caught me by the back buttons on my dress and pulled me aside.

"Can you up shut your mouth?" he asked.

"Yes sir," I nodded, knowing it wouldn't be wise to correct him.

"Then, you can make the greetings at the door. But with good manners," he added.

"Here," he said, "you practice with your opa." He stood in the archway between the parlor and the kitchen. He motioned for me to pretend there was a door between us.

"K-nock, K-nock, K-nock," he pantomimed with his fist.

I was ready and waiting.

"Halloooooo," Opa imitated, the bashful way Bert always did. "This evening, I come to see Katherine. Is she at home?"

"Oh, Mr. Goodner," I said, remembering my manners, "it's so nice to see you." Then without a moment's hesitation, "Are you going to marry my sister?"

"Nein, nein, nein," Opa answered. But before we could try it again, Bert Goodner was pulling into the yard in one of the fanciest buggies I'd ever seen.

"Oh, please, Opa," I begged, "please let me answer the door."

"No monkey works," Opa replied sharply.

"It's monkey business," I told him. "Oh, all right, no monkey business. I promise."

A moment later, I opened the door to find Bert Goodner standing there in his best Sunday suit, hair all slicked back, crumpled felt hat in one hand, and a strangled bouquet of zinnias in the other.

Much to my great disappointment there wasn't any sparking done on our front porch that night. And from my spot behind the hydrangea bush, I couldn't even tell if they did any spooning either. It was real romantic, though. The two of them sat there on our porch with the moonlight shining through the fir tree. Bert brought along his banjo, and he picked out a tune for Katherine. His deep baritone voice was smooth and sure of itself as he sang.

"I've got an old mule and her name is Sal. Fifteen years on the Erie Canal." Katherine joined him on the choruses. "Low bridge, everybody down, low bridge, we're coming to a town. You can always tell your neighbor, you can always tell your pal, if you've ever navigated on the Erie Canal."

I was all set to join in on the next chorus when I felt a sharp pain on my left ear. Before I knew it, Opa took hold of my earlobe, hauled me to my feet, and marched me into the house.

"Oww-eee," I started to say until his hand

clamped over my mouth. The next thing I knew, he whacked his cane across the backs of my calves and sent me upstairs to bed.

"No more dropping the eaves," Opa said under his breath.

"It's eavesdropping, Opa," I told him.

"Dropping the eaves, eavesdropping. No matter what it is, to bed you go."

I couldn't see a blasted thing from the bedroom window, but I could hear them singing, so I sat there in my nightgown at the end of the bed and sang right along with them on the next song.

"Then dance the boat-man dance. O dance the boat-man dance. We danced all night 'til broad daylight, go home with the girls in the mornin'. Oh high row, the boat men row. Floatin' down the river, the O-hi-o."

Bert stayed for a little while longer. I listened for their voices, but could only hear mumblings every now and again. I heard him harness up his horse and as he pulled away from the yard, I heard him singing. "Sittin' in the moonlight, June light, moonlight. Sittin' in the moonlight, rah-do-dah."

Katherine was as quiet as a mouse when she came to bed. I pretended I was asleep until she almost had her pajamas pulled over her head.

"Tell me! Tell me! Tell me!" I said, jumping up

to my knees in the middle of the bed. "Did he kiss
you? Did he kiss you?"

"OOOOOh," Katherine cried out. "Callie, don't
you ever do that again. You nearly scared the socks
right off me!"

"Well, did he?"

"I'm not someone to kiss and tell, Callie Common. And you shouldn't either. Of course, I will say
this. There's nothing to tell."

"Oh phooey!" I said disappointedly. "I was hoping you could tell me what it's like to be kissed."

"No, dear little sister. Eventually that's for me to
know and you to find out, but at this moment, I'm
afraid I can't enlighten you. Maybe I'll be able to
next time," she said. "You'll be the first to know."
And there was just enough moonlight to see her
wink at me.

No one slept late that next morning or for the
whole next week. We had break-your-back chores
to get ready for the Sorghum Festival. In only a
week's time, we'd have to have our vegetables
picked from Mama's kitchen garden, our butter,
eggs, and cheeses ready and the handmades finished to sell out of the back of our wagon. I loved
going to the Sorghum Festival since we'd go into

town early on that Saturday morning and spend the whole day, at least until it was milking time.

Katherine still hadn't heard any word about the teaching job in District #12. My own school was about to start, and Katherine promised to ride me to school the first day if she was still home. While we worked on a list of chores as long as your arm, Katherine helped me with my words for the big spelling bee. That was only one of the other reasons I loved the Sorghum Festival so much. Every year Landry's Sorghum Mill would invite all the people in the county to bring in their sorghum. Then one whole day, the mill would grind the sorghum brought in and cook it down into syrup. Each person there could take home a jug of fresh-made syrup. The festival always had a pie-eating contest, a pig judging, a box-lunch raffle, and a spelling bee. I loved to hear the fiddle players as they tuned up for the big barn dance in the evening. And this year, I wanted to try one more time for the spelling bee. Last year, I'd only made alternate, but I thought I could do better.

"Nomination," Katherine said as she carefully yanked on the green leaves of a carrot and watched it pull away, orange and whiskery from the dirt.

"N-O-M-I-N-A-T-I-O-N," I answered, standing in between rows of sweet peppers and beets with a four-tined shovel in my hand.

"Wrong," she said crossly. "Take your seat, Calista," she imitated in her best teacher voice.

"What's wrong? That's how you spell it," I retorted.

"Yes, Miss Smarty Pants, but you forgot to repeat your word, before and after."

"Oh frog legs," I groaned.

"Oh frog legs, nothing. If you jump in there and spell the word, then you'll be wrong."

"Nomination. N-O-M-I-N-A-T-I-O-N, nomination."

"Right," Katherine said this time, only with a smile. And before I knew it, she'd rattled off four or five more words from our Alexander speller as though she'd memorized them.

After we finished with the carrots and beets, we each grabbed a handle of the bushel basket and carried it over to the back porch. Baskets full of turban squash, purple cabbages, onions, and carrots lined the walls. Opa was sitting on the back step finishing a new harness.

Katherine was a true taskmaster. She ran me through "recitation, embellish, discipline" and half a dozen other words before she let me take a break that evening.

Even the next morning, Katherine was relentless.

"Here, Callie, take the reins," Katherine offered on the way to school. "Fanny's so gentle, she won't hurt you, especially when she's harnessed up to the cart the way she is."

"No-sir-ee-bob," I answered and shook my head. "You're doing an exceptionally fine job of driving Fanny."

"You know, Callie," Katherine started in, "one of these days you're gonna have to get over your fear of horses."

"You'd have a fear of horses, too, Katherine Common, if you'd been pinned in a stall by a horse and had two of your ribs broke." Even thinking about that day when I was only five years old made the ache come back to my chest. Truth was, I thought I was sometimes more afraid of being pinned again than I was of the pain.

"The way to conquer your fears is to face them."

I stared at Katherine and wrinkled my eyes at her. "Is that a maxim you learned in school?"

"No, Callie. I didn't learn that in school. It's just something I know. So here," she said, trying to put the reins in my hands, "now's the best time to start."

I pushed the reins away. "I'll start tomorrow," I told her. "Maybe next week. Or the week after. I'm not gonna put myself any closer to a horse until I'm good and ready."

Before another quarter of a mile had gone by, Katherine started up her list of words again.

"Obtrusive," Katherine ordered.

"Goodness, you're bossy," I replied.

"That's what it takes to be a good teacher," she answered.

Fanny was clipping and clopping along with a gentle sway.

"You'd make a good teacher, Callie. You're just bossy enough to make a fine teacher someday."

"Oh really?"

"It takes a little bit of bossy, a whole lot of heart, a ton of smarts, and a passel of courage to be a good teacher," Katherine explained.

"Well, don't forget spunk," I added. "And gump- tion, too. And while you're at it, throw in a little fortitude, an ounce or two of patience, and a heap of dedication."

We rode in silence for a few moments. Having Katherine tell me I was bossy was one thing, but having Katherine tell me I might make a good teacher was another matter altogether.

"You really think I'd make a good teacher?" I asked, not waiting for her answer. "That's work I'd surely like to do. Me, Calista Marie Common, Schoolteacher."

"Schoolteacher," Katherine ordered.

"What?"

"Schoolteacher. Spell it!"

"Good heavens. Schoolteacher, S-C-H-O-O-L-T-E-A-C-H-E-R, schoolteacher. So there!"

I did fine until Katherine started giving me words like "llama, indignant, and calendar."

"Where did those come from?" I finally asked.

"The back of the book," was all she said, and without missing a beat, she gave me "incessantly."

"Are you gonna make a box supper for the raffle?" I asked in between words.

"I haven't decided yet."

I made a face she couldn't see.

"Well, if you do, you know you'll have to sit with whomever buys it."

Katherine still didn't bother to answer me.

"You might want to put in a mess of biscuits. Bert likes your biscuits, in case you don't remember."

"I'll thank you to mind your own business, Callie," was all she said.

"He's a lot older than you, isn't he?"

"What of it?" she answered smartly. "Mama always did say 'Age is Wisdom.' "

"I heard Velma Nicholson say he's twenty-nine years old on his next birthday and if you ask me, that's O-L-D."

"Nobody asked you, Callie. At least I'm lucky

enough to have a caller. Some girls end up old maids."

"Well, Katherine, exactly what are you gonna do if Bert wants to do more than call on you? What if Bert proposes? Are you gonna S-W-O-O-N and answer with your heart or your head, the way the ladies do in the R-O-M-A-N-C-E books?"

There was a long pause from Katherine, and we both sat there in silence. We saw the schoolhouse come slowly into view.

"Believe me, Callie, I wish I knew. He's the nicest, sweetest man I ever met. But he *is* a whole lot older than I am. And to be honest, I don't know if I love him or not."

"Maybe you're not old enough. Maybe fifteen's too soon to know if you love another person. Look at me. I'm twelve, and I don't love anyone yet. Maybe you have to be sixteen or seventeen to really know how to L-O-V-E someone."

"Whatever it is, I don't have an answer," she replied. "And Mama's not here to help me. Besides, if I get the teacher's job, teachers can't marry anyway, and I'd rather be a teacher for a little while to see if I like it."

There was no more time for talk. The schoolhouse was nearly in front of us, and I was late. I hopped down from the wagon and started to hurry in.

"Callie," Katherine hollered, as I jumped onto the porch. I turned to look at her. "Awkward," she ordered.

"Awkward, A-W-K-W-A-R-D, awkward!" I hollered back, before my voice was drowned out by the clanging of the school bell.

Rumor had it that Mr. Dreyfus was the meanest schoolteacher in all of Hamilton County. But whether he was mean or not, our school had won the spelling bee at the Sorghum Festival for as long as anyone could remember. By Thursday of the first week we'd already had four spelling drills. By Friday, we were ready to find out who would represent the school at the spelling bee on Saturday.

All twelve students from the Bakers Corner School, District #8 were standing in front of the room. I took a spot between Esco Pitts and Harriet Fancher.

Mr. Dreyfus pulled his Alexander speller off the pile of books on his desk and flipped to a page toward the middle.

"Oh, no," I whispered to Esco. He started to shake his head.

"That's it. My goose is cooked. I'm done for," he moaned. "I don't know any of those words. I might as well sit down right now," he whispered. He stuck his hands in his overall pockets and stared at his shoes.

Mr. Dreyfus had drilled us on spelling every day and I figured if I could keep up with the older students, it might come down to me and Harriet and maybe Orin Toliver.

Poor Esco went down like a stone in a pool of water after his first word, but he sat at his desk and cheered the others on. He climbed halfway out of his seat with excitement when he knew a word and a student still standing didn't. Words like alcohol, curtain, and continent felt as easy as pie that afternoon and within twenty minutes there were only four of us left. Orin Toliver, Jess Comstock, me and Harriet.

Jess stumbled on embellish, and I was instantly glad that Katherine had been so strict with me when we practiced that morning.

When it was my turn again, Mr. Dreyfus gave me "business." I hesitated for a few seconds until I remembered one of the tricks Katherine told me.

"Remember there's 'sin' in the middle of business," she offered.

"Business, B-U ... S-I-N ... E-S-S, business," I spelled.

It finally came down to me and Harriet. We spelled out our words, clear and strong. The whole room was so silent you could've heard a pin drop.

"Isthmus, Harriet. An isthmus is a body of land with water on three sides."

"Isthmus. I-S-T-H-M-U-S, isthmus."

My hands were already a little clammy and cold, but when I saw Mr. Dreyfus flip toward the back of the speller, my heart skipped a beat and Harriet's eyes got as big as fifty-cent pieces.

The two of us stumbled through prescription, principles, and scrupulous, but subterranean was Harriet's undoing.

"Subterranean," she repeated slowly. "S-U-B," she started and then paused. "T-I-R-A-N-I-A-N, subterranean."

While Harriet made her way to her seat, I stood there in front of the class, feeling like the loneliest person in the whole wide world. But more than anything, I was trying to wrack my brain for a spelling clue Katherine had taught me.

"We stand on old 'terra firma,' " she'd told me as one of her clues. I tried to put her hint into use.

"Subterranean, Callie," Mr. Dreyfus repeated.

"Subterranean." I paused to try and get my brain organized for a minute.

"Are you gonna spell the word, or are we gonna wait for the sun to rise and set one more time."

"Yes sir," I answered. I took a big breath and crossed both fingers behind my back.

"Subterranean. S-U-B . . . T-E-R-R-A . . . N-E-A-N, subterranean."

As soon as Mr. Dreyfus said, "Absolutely correct," the whole room burst into applause and cheers. My face blushed beet red as Esco and Harriet came up to congratulate me. Everyone was supportive except for one person.

"Mr. Dreyfus, Mr. Dreyfus," Orin Toliver called out. "I think it's ridiculous, Mr. Dreyfus," Orin said.

"What's that, Orin?"

"I thought only boys could be representatives for the spelling bee, Mr. Dreyfus. Seems to me there's not much good to sending a girl."

"Oh?" Mr. Dreyfus said, raising his eyebrows. "And how's that Mr. Toliver?"

"Well, sir, what good's a girl? Seems to me we ought to be sendin' a boy. Boys are smarter. Boys are better."

"Mr. Toliver," Mr. Dreyfus started to say in a voice he used only once in a while, and when he did, it sent chills down our spines. He wasted no time walking over to Orin's desk and standing within a few inches of him. "That's correct, Mr. Toliver, we could send a boy to the spelling bee." Then Mr. Dreyfus leaned over, right up close to Orin's face. "But it appears that the smartest and best spellers in this school are girls. Spelled, G-I-R-

L-S! So, Orin Toliver, put that in your pipe and smoke it." Mr. Dreyfus turned around and walked over to me.

"Calista Marie Common," he said, and I popped up out of my seat.

"This is for you, the best speller and the very best representative from the Bakers Corner School at the Boxley Sorghum Festival." Then he pinned a piece of blue ribbon with a hand-lettered button onto my school dress. Up to that day, I never ever remembered feeling so proud.

CHAPTER EIGHT

My Alexander Speller

"Katherine, Katherine," I called out breathlessly as I raced up to the house and through the door on the back porch. "I did it! I did it!" Katherine had not been at school to pick me up with Fanny, so I'd nearly run the whole four miles home. Not finding her in the house, I ran out to the chicken coop and not finding her there, I headed out to the barn.

"Katherine! Opa! Where are you?"

"Over here," I heard Opa say. I looked by the grain bins and the calf pens and finally found him milking Hester, our cow.

"Opa, I did it," I told him, all in a sweat.

"And what is it you did?" he asked with a smile.

"I'm the representative for the schoolhouse to the spelling bee tomorrow!" I leaned over to show him my pin. Hester even turned her head to watch us.

Opa let go of the teats for a second. He squinted

his eyes and looked at my badge, giving it a careful inspection.

"My goodness," he said thoughtfully, "very official you are."

"Where's Katherine?" I asked. "I want to show her." I looked around the barn and stood over by the big double doors, thinking maybe I could see her out in the garden.

"Katherine is gone," he answered. "Michael came for her this morning to take her to the schoolteacher interview. The superintendent is making her rounds tomorrow and wants to talk to her. Three girls are interviewing. Katherine packed her nicest dress. She stays at Aunt Mary's house for the night."

Opa chuckled a little and put his hat back on his head. He patted Hester on the rump, and she turned to look at him once more, chomping on a mouthful of hay. "And Katherine was nervous as a fish. Never before have I seen her like that. This job she wants so very much."

Opa hung the milking stool on the wall and picked up the pail filled with chalky white milk. He poured a little bit into an old tin cake pan. Cats and kittens came scurrying from every corner of the barn the minute the first splash of milk hit the bottom of the pan.

"She is only gone for this one afternoon, and I miss her," he said wistfully. "And her biscuits. They are waiting to go into her box supper for the festival," he told me. "What should we do?"

"Why, we'll take her box supper in with us tomorrow. I know she'd want us to. I'm sure of it. I know we'll see her tomorrow at the Sorghum Festival, won't we?" I asked.

"Of course we will. She can't miss seeing you in the bee spelling."

"Opa," I said, laughing a little and taking his hand as we walked back to the house, "it's *spelling . . . bee.*"

"Spelling bee, spelling bee," he repeated. "Back to front, I get my words, don't I?"

"Ja, mein Liebchen," I teased.

After dinner, we finished loading the wagon and Opa sat by lamplight in the kitchen putting tongue oil on the new harness he hoped to sell. I sat at the table and wrote my spelling words over and over on the chalkboard. I concentrated on the words at the end of the book. Magnanimity, conscientious, feudal, dexterity, discourtesy, harmonious.

Opa looked up every now and again while I muttered and sputtered over the words.

"What's it about an old dog?" he asked.

I looked at him with furrowed brows.

"Teaching the old dog like me?" he asked again.

"Oh," I said, realizing what he meant, "you can't teach an old dog new tricks. Is that it, Opa? Who says you're an old dog?"

"Everybody!" he replied. "But this old dog wants to learn the English." He rubbed oil along the reins roughly as he spoke. "I think it is time I learned the English." He looked up. "You teach me the English, Callie?" he asked. "You think this old dog, the English, he can learn?"

"Of course, Opa," I told him.

"Although," he said thoughtfully, "I have wondered many times about this English language."

"What's that, Opa?"

"I wonder to myself and say, 'Not one single umlaut. Johannes Kreuzer, how can you learn a language that does not use the umlaut?' "

"Oh, don't worry about that, Opa. I can teach you." I hopped down from the chair and lit a candle to take up to my room. "We'll make a great team, absolutely and positively." I kissed him on the cheek and headed out the back door toward the outhouse. I sat out there with a candle and my Alexander speller and turned to page 139. Illegible, ingenuous, perseverance, conspicuous, emigrant, partition, and dessert.

Knock. Knock. Knock.

I nearly jumped a mile.

"Are you in there?" I heard Opa ask.

"Yes sir," I said loudly through the door.

"Should I hitch up the horse to pull you out?" Opa asked.

"No, Opa," I answered. "I didn't fall in."

Up in the bedroom, I put on my nightgown. I set the candle on the nightstand and propped my pillow on the headboard so I could see my speller. I turned to page 146. Autobiography, convenience, escort, contralto, and discriminate.

Between pages 146 and 147, I heard a strange shuffling sound on the stairs.

"Grrrrrr," I heard.

"Opa?"

There was no answer.

"Rrrrrrraaaaaarrrrrrrh," I heard as I put my book down on my lap.

"Opa?" I called out.

"Rrrah, rrrraah, rrraaaaah," rumbled from the doorway. A figure covered in an old dark wool blanket lumbered into the room. "A wild brown bear is loose from the circus," I heard a muffled voice say.

"Opa? Opa?" and I dove under the covers.

"Raaaah," the bear cried.

"AAAAAAAAAAH," I screamed. "It's a bear! It's a bear!"

"So hungry the bear is for arms, tonight," I heard and I felt paws grabbing along the covers wherever I moved.

"No! No! Not my arms," I shouted for all I was worth.

"So hungry I am for the legs of little girls," I heard the voice exclaim, and I screamed even more as I heard the bear growling and growling.

Then suddenly, the growling stopped.

"Opa?" I mumbled from underneath the covers. "Opa?" I flipped the covers over my head and saw Opa sitting on the edge of the bed. He was winded and could barely get his breath, his hand on his chest.

"Do you need one of your heart pills?" I asked.

All he could do was nod. I reached into his vest pocket, took out the small vial, and found a tiny white pill.

"Here," I commanded, handing him the tiny pill. He put it under his tongue and sat quietly. I patted him on the back and smoothed his wild hair down a little bit. The pill took effect so quickly that he was able to take a deep breath before long and speak.

"Perhaps I am not so young as I thought," he said with a little smile. "You take such good care of your old opa," he told me.

I spread the extra blanket on the bed.

"My, my," he said, standing by the end of the

bed, "such a sky full of winking, twinkling stars tonight, Callie." I knelt at the bottom and looked out the window with him. We searched for Orion's Belt together.

"You see, even now, the three of us can be together," he told me. I nodded in agreement. He hugged me, then gave me a kiss on the forehead. I watched as he left the room to go downstairs.

I climbed under the covers and noticed for the first time how empty the big bed felt without Katherine. I squirmed and twisted. I tried sleeping on my stomach. I tried sleeping on my back. I tossed. I turned. I felt so alone.

Finally, I hopped out of bed and tiptoed downstairs. I went into Mama's room and took an old nightgown off the hook from the back of the door. I carefully opened the dresser drawer, where I knew Papa kept his flannel shirts, and I tiptoed back upstairs.

In my room, the smell of Papa's old flannel shirt was like new mown hay and the scent of rosewater was on Mama's gown as I slipped it over my head. I took Papa's shirt and wrapped it around my pillow. I took my Alexander speller and propped it open to page 143, to what I thought was the hardest page in the whole book. I tucked the big folds of Mama's nightie all around me and pulled the covers up to my chin. Antecedent, declension, advantageous, complacence, subjugation. Like layers of a sandwich, I placed my Alexander speller, opened up, on the bed. Then I put my pillow covered in Papa's shirt on top of the speller. Finally, I turned my head and lay down on the pillow, so the words could come right up through the pillow and in my left ear. I nestled my head farther down into the feathery mass. Bed. Speller. Pillow. My Ear. In the darkness, I waited for the words to lift off the page and start seeping in.

I fell asleep that night reciting propitious, perilous, and picturesque and hoped the words would be glued like wallpaper to the insides of my brain by morning.

The Saturday of the Sorghum Festival dawned bright and beautiful, a lovely mid-October day. I awoke to hear the sound of Opa huffing and puffing in the yard. When I looked out the window, I saw the big kettle for cleaning chickens on the fire outside. Already filled with water, the steaming kettle was bubbling. Then I saw Opa. He was a sight, chasing around the side of the chicken coop with a hatchet held high above his head, his hair all gone wild and six ways to Sunday.

"Hühnchen, Hühnchen. Kommt her, meine Hühnchen," he said enticingly. He kept making a clucking sound way down in his throat. But the birds always stayed just enough steps ahead of him to be out of his reach. Round and round the chicken coop they went, Opa and the frightened, clucking chickens. When it came to chickens, Mama was a neck-wringer, and Opa was a hatcheter. Either way, I didn't care much for being around when the job was done. Four not-so-lucky hens were already tied to the fence by their feet and missing their heads.

"English, Opa!" I called from the window. "Speak English," I shouted. "The chickens will understand you better, if you speak English."

I bolted out of bed and put on my best dress and apron. I tied a green ribbon in my hair, washed my face in the basin, and dashed downstairs.

Katherine's box supper was stuffed so full of biscuits I could hardly get the lid to stay down. I tucked a fistful of butter-colored, tulip tree leaves under the string. We finished loading the wagon, and I climbed up onto the seat next to Opa with my Alexander speller in my hand. The ride into town took us nearly an hour, since our wagon was packed to the gills with goods to sell, and we couldn't hurry Fanny. By the time we'd put in our small haul of sweet sorghum, there was barely room for the bushels of squash, purple cabbages, and six dressed chickens in a basket.

"I'll never understand how a 'dressed chicken'

can be naked," I said to Opa as I sat down. Opa climbed in beside me and tucked the new harnesses in an old pillowcase under the buckboard by his feet.

Long before we got into town, our noses caught the pungent smoke and sweet smell of boiling sorghum. Landry's Sorghum Mill was the one and only big building in Boxley. As we rolled in past the dry goods store and the post office, Mr. Comstock was hoisting the flag. We pulled the wagon alongside the loading dock at the mill, and a man came to help Opa unload the sorghum so that it could be pressed out into juice and then cooked down to syrup. Two brown mules were already walking lazy circles around the sorghum press by the woodshed, and a vat of syrup as big as a water trough was on the boil and cooking down. Little boys kept putting small sticks under the fire. From time to time, one of the boys would throw a buckeye or two into the flames, and pretty soon those buckeyes would give a big POP when they burst open.

I stood on the wagon seat, looking out over Boxley Corners.

"Picturesque, P-I-C-T-U-R-E-S-Q-U-E, picturesque," I practiced as I jumped down. I just knew with all my heart this was going to be the best day ever.

CHAPTER NINE

The Sorghum Festival

"For such good helping," Opa told me, and he pressed a nickel into the palm of my right hand. He kissed me smack in the middle of the forehead. I knew that while he was busy selling things from the wagon, I was on my own for a while.

Opa moved the wagon over by the post office and had barely set the handbrake before someone wanted to buy a few of his orange-and-green-striped turban squash. Opa began his wheeling and dealing, speaking half in English and half in German, he was so excited. I was free as a bird to wander about the tiny crossroads of Boxley that day. I made a beeline for the porch on the second story of the dry goods store. I could see from corner to corner, and I looked for Katherine. I was hoping she'd already be there, but I checked every square foot of the crossroads. There was no sign of her.

"I'm gonna go and buy me a sorghum cookie," I

called to Esco Pitts on the way down the steps. "Want to come along?"

Ladies from the Friends' Church always sold baked goods. We eyed a table full of sorghum taffy, cookies, and crystal sorghum candies. The smell was thick and sweet.

"I'll have me one of those," I said, pointing to a cookie about as big as a saucer. "The kind with the store-bought sugar sprinkled on top, if you please."

"You're in luck today," the church lady told us. "They're two for a penny." I shared mine with Esco.

We strolled past Fleener's boardinghouse and peeked in the tent where we saw Mr. Blanchard using a long cane to walk one of his black-and-white, Poland China pigs around the show ring.

"Well, hello, Callie," Mrs. Fancher said when we saw her by the post office.

"That's some sewing basket," I told her, as she held it up for me to see. "Red satin lining and everything," I said, touching it with my finger.

"I've never had one this elegant," she explained. "Seems as though I'm gonna have to sew us pretty elegant clothes from now on."

Pastor Greene nearly scared the socks right off me when he came up behind us as we watched the start of the pie-eating contest.

"Don't be late for the spelling bee, Callie," he warned.

"Oh no sir," I answered, after I'd caught my breath again.

"Once they get the box suppers raffled off, we'll get started."

"How soon will that be?" I asked, and without answering, Pastor Greene pointed beyond the platform set up in the center of the crossroads, where we could see a dozen young ladies buzzing around the tables.

"Come on, Esco," I said, "I have to take Katherine's box supper over there."

Without a doubt, Katherine's box simply looked like the very best one. Harriet had come along by then, and all three of us found a sunny spot over on the church steps where we had a good view of the raffle.

"Does Marie Louise have a box supper in there, too?" I asked Harriet as we watched the boxes being lined up.

"She surely does," Harriet answered. "She spent the better part of the morning decorating it, too."

I kept looking for Katherine, but I still hadn't seen her. Every so often, I stood up on the steps and peered around the crowd.

Mr. Comstock from the dry goods store served as auctioneer. Half a dozen young ladies stood by the table giggling and whispering to each other. He clanged a triangle, the kind used to call people to dinner. The noise was loud and clear and brought people over to the table.

"Now look at this," and he held up a box wrapped in brown paper and tied on top with a twine bow, "we have our first box supper, ladies and gentlemen, which, I might add, smells mighty good." Mr. Comstock put his nose up to the paper and took in a big whiff. "Fried chicken, I'd say, and maybe a piece of apple pie from what I can tell."

"Fried chicken and that's a piece of apple *walnut* pie. Can't you read, Harold Comstock?" one of the young women said, and everyone in the crowd laughed. Mr. Comstock put on his glasses and looked at the list written on the side of the box. "Oh, so it is. Apple *walnut* pie," he admitted.

"Who'll start off the bidding?" he asked.

"I forgot to write down the stuff in the box," I whispered to Harriet. "What am I gonna do now?"

"Don't worry about it, it'll be all right."

"Twenty cents," someone hollered, and the box-supper raffle was off and running. The bidding quickly moved to twenty-five cents and most of the box suppers were going for forty or forty-five cents. Marie Louise's box went to Mr. Comstock's oldest son, Emmett, and Marie Louise blushed as deep as a rose. Then Mr. Comstock held up Katherine's box.

"Well, I'll tell you, folks," and Mr. Comstock was really grinning, "this box is a real two-hander." He acted as though he could barely hold up the box. Then he gave it his usual nose test and said, "Unless my sniffer is wrong, this smells like hamloaf."

"Hamloaf with a little spicy mustard," I stood up and hollered without thinking. "Oops," I said suddenly as I put my hand over my mouth and sat down. Everyone in the crowd laughed. "Oh mercy," I whispered to Harriet, "I wish Katherine was here."

"Probably a nice hunk of hamloaf, a few of those sweet bread 'n' butter pickles." He jostled the box a bit with both hands. "And judging from the weight of it, at least a half a dozen biscuits," then he smelled the corner one more time, "and without a doubt, there's a hint of strawberry-rhubarb jam coming out of this box, too."

I stood up one more time and looked all around for Katherine, but she was nowhere to be found.

"Let's be sporting here and start this one off at twenty-five cents, shall we?"

"Thirty," a voice hollered. I recognized Bert's deep voice.

"I'll make that thirty-five," Mr. Fancher's oldest

boy said, looking over his shoulder at me and winking.

"Forty!"

"Brisk business here, folks, I do believe. Will anyone make it fifty?" Mr. Comstock asked, and there
was a long silence.

"Fifty," came a reply from over by the horseshoe
pitching. All the heads turned. The voice came
from a group of Sheridan people. I was getting
nervous since I knew it was customary for the person who made the box supper to sit with whomever
bought it. I didn't want to see Katherine have to sit
with a stranger.

There was another long pause in the bidding,
then Mr. Comstock said, "Fifty cents. Going once,
going twice," but before he could get out any more,
Bert's big booming voice interrupted him.

"One dollar," he called and everyone turned
around to take a look at him, standing there in his
leather apron. The whole crowd smiled and a few
people whistled.

"Sold," Mr. Comstock answered quickly. Bert
took a dollar bill out of his pants pocket and ac-
cepted the box from Mr. Comstock. He walked over
to the blacksmith's shop and sat on a bench by the
door.

"You better go tell him Katherine's not here,"
Harriet said, nearly pushing me down the steps.

Bert was starting to untie the box when I stepped up in front of him.

"Mr. Goodner, sir," I squeaked.

"Why hello, Callie," he said pleasantly. "I've been keeping an eye out for Katherine this morning. But I haven't seen her yet."

"No sir, we haven't either." I grabbed onto the hitching post and was glad for a place to put my hands.

"Is she coming at all today?"

"I wish I knew," I answered honestly.

"I almost hate to eat this without Katherine. She might show up. Why don't you keep me company?" He patted the bench and opened the box. "I'm awfully hungry."

So there we sat on the blacksmith bench, Bert Goodner and me, and me with my short legs that didn't even reach the ground. I watched him eat the whole sandwich in just a few bites, then he finished the pickles. In the blink of an eye, he'd devoured all six biscuits.

"Katherine's a mighty good cook," he said as he took his bandanna and used it like a napkin. "Will you tell her," he started to say, but Harriet came running over to me.

"Come on, Callie," she said breathlessly, "they're looking for you. They want to start the spelling bee." She grabbed my hand.

*   *   *

Pastor Greene lined us up alphabetically. I stood next to Cynthia Gravatt from Sheridan. She'd been last year's winner. While Pastor Greene was reminding us about the rules, I caught sight of a buggy coming up to the Boxley crossroads. I squinted to make sure it was who I thought it was.

Part of me heard what Pastor Greene was saying, but the other part of me was looking toward Opa. I caught his eye and pointed toward the road.

"Callie, are you listening?" Pastor Greene asked.

"Yes sir," I answered.

I wiped my hands down the front of my dress to take the sweat off them and tried to make sure I listened to the rest of what Pastor Greene had to say. Tragedy was my first word, and I spelled it correctly. I let myself look out toward the road again. Aunt Mary was in the buggy, sure enough, but where was Katherine? I leaned up close to Cynthia to get a better look.

"Callie," Pastor Greene said crossly. I vaguely heard Cynthia get her next word as I saw Aunt Mary walk right up to Opa. They had angry words, I could tell from the looks on their faces and by the way they were talking to each other. Opa started to get all red in the face, and he moved back toward

the wagon and grabbed onto the side to steady himself. I was just about to step out of line when I
heard Pastor Greene call out my name again.

"Callie, your word is discipline. Discipline means
knowledge."

As I watched Aunt Mary spit more words at Opa,
I saw him put his hand up to his chest. He seemed
to be gasping for breath. His face was flushed.

"Callie," Pastor Greene snapped. I took my eyes
off Opa only for a second.

"D-I-S-C-I-P-L-I-N-E, there, I spelled it," I said.
Easy as pie, I remember thinking at the time.

"That's incorrect, Callie," Pastor Greene said,
sounding very apologetic.

"But that's how you spell it," I argued.

"True, but you forgot to repeat the word before
and after. I'm sorry. You're disqualified. You'll
have to step down."

I didn't wait to hear another word, but jumped
off the front of the stand and ran over to Opa. Two
men were helping him sit, and Herr Baumeister
was fanning him with his hat.

"Where are your pills?"

Opa was in so much pain, he couldn't even speak.

I searched in his vest pockets. I found the little
vial in one of them. I quickly tucked a pill under his
tongue. He closed his eyes and within a few sec-

onds, the muscles in his face began to relax. Herr Baumeister kept on fanning Opa. I unbuttoned Opa's top collar button.

He eventually patted my hand, and I breathed a big sigh of relief.

"That was a bad one, wasn't it?"

"Ja, I get myself all worked up," he said, still a bit breathlessly. "And now, my head. I think it will split open with the aching."

"Did Aunt Mary upset you?"

"Ach ja, that old bitty. She upsets me. Like a thorn in my side, she is."

"What did she say?"

"She says Katherine does not come home."

"What do you mean, Opa?" I watched Opa pull at the collar of his shirt to loosen the opening a little more. He was taking in regular breaths now, and his face had a more normal color to it.

"She says Katherine did not get the teacher's job." Opa stamped his foot on the ground. "That woman, so angry she makes me. She says Katherine stays at the boardinghouse to cook and wash. Mary says she starts Katherine today. Katherine cannot even come today to the celebration."

"Tell Aunt Mary to send Katherine home, Opa," I said.

"Ja, I would, but Mary says Katherine wants to stay and work." Opa took out his handkerchief and mopped his brow. "I am torn," Opa said. "I do not want Katherine to work for Mary, but we could use the money to pay the funeral bills. My Katerina, she knows this."

"When will we see Katherine?"

"That is a good question, mein Kleines. That Mary, she's a driver of slaves."

"It's slave driver, Opa."

"Slave driver, then. I am thinking right now we could have enough money by Christmas. Then our Katherine could come home."

"Do we really need the money?"

"A lot I will have to think on this," Opa said finally. "Until Christmas, we will do this, and then Katherine is home again. I cannot bear the thought of my Katerina working for a driver of slaves."

Herr Baumeister helped Opa stand up, and they found a bench on the porch of the dry goods store.

"Maybe we should go straight home," I said.

"Nein," Opa replied. "Not until you win the bee spelling."

"Oh, Opa," I said, remembering it for the first time since I saw him put his hand up to his chest, "I'm such a disappointment to you. I didn't win it at all. I made a mistake and was disqualified." I could feel the tears start to well up in my eyes.

"Now, now, Herzchen," he said, rubbing my arm. "This bee spelling doesn't matter. There is always

next year. Here, mein Herzchen, don't cry," and he
handed me his handkerchief.

"Maybe it is time to go," he said to Herr Baumeister. "Enough we have done here today." He took a
wad of money out of his pocket and licked his thumb
and forefinger as he started to count the bills. "Einundzwanzig, zweiundzwanzig, dreiundzwanzig,
vierundzwanzig," he said. "Little by little, we have
enough for the undertaker."

"I'll get our sorghum," I told Opa, and he met
me by the mill. I put the gallon jug in the back of
the wagon and climbed in. Even Fanny looked sad
going home. Her ears were back and her step was
all slow and uneasy. And me, I felt like I'd got the
wind kicked out of me. I sat next to Opa, and he
put his arm around me. Even though that was a
comfort, I wanted Katherine to come home. I
wanted Papa to come home. And more than anything, I wanted Mama.

CHAPTER TEN

The Huckster

In only a few weeks' time, the better part of our fall work was finished. Opa and I had buried most of the apples under layers of straw. We'd turned the cabbages upside down and hung them from the ceiling of the root cellar and covered the red cabbages with cloths to hold their sweetness. We'd filled seven five-gallon crocks with sauerkraut and moved them to the darkest part of the springhouse, along with the potatoes and carrots.

"Do you think the egg barrel needs more sawdust and straw?" Opa asked me one afternoon. I put my hand down into the barrel to check the sawdust, and when I did, I felt a long slithery thing.

"AAAAAAAAAHH!" I screamed. Opa, sober-faced, reached into the barrel and pulled up a long thin snake! I put my hands up in front of my face and heard a hissing sound. I watched from between my fingers as it jiggled and jumped around.

"AAAAAAAHHH!" I screamed again.

"Schlange! Schlange!" Opa hollered. I heard hissing and I watched the snake go flying across the room. I jumped.

An old piece of rope lay on the floor nearly five feet from the spot where I'd leaped away.

"Ha, ha, ha," Opa laughed. "I have gotten you with the snake once again. A cat so scared you are," he chuckled.

"Oh, Opa, you're mean to tease me like that." I patted my chest and tried to catch my breath. "And it's scaredy-cat, anyway," I said, beginning to feel a little better.

"Snakes won't hurt you, at least not the ones made of rope," he said, chuckling. We both heard the sound of a wagon coming into the yard at the same time.

We stepped out of the dark springhouse into the bright sunlight to find a huckster's wagon pulling into the barnyard. LESTER BREWSTER SUNDRY ITEMS MISHAWAKA, INDIANA was written on the side of the wagon. The clipping and clopping of the huckster's horse and the clanking of the pots and pans and paraphernalia tied to the sides sounded like a musical band had arrived. The horse was a dapple-gray filly and had a cluster of deep purple feathers hooked to her bridle. I pulled my sweater closer around me, and Opa stopped at the pump by the back door to get a bucket of water for the horse.

"Hello, hello," the huckster said to us, tipping his hat. "How are you all on this fine October day?"

"Sehr gut," Opa answered in German. I looked at him and remembered how he tended to use his English only when he wanted to.

"I've got lots of bargains for you," the huckster told us. I caught myself staring at the man's green plaid pants and shoes, so shiny you could almost see your face reflected in them. He wore a dandy bowler hat and wide, forest green suspenders. His black tie was knotted in a natty bow and the curls on his handlebar mustache were perfectly waxed in circles the size of quarters.

"Lester Brewster's the name. Most people call me Les with the Best," he said in a kind of patter like he was going to do a fancy dance step or recite a long poem. I watched as he waltzed around the wagon, opening drawers and doors, setting up his wares to show them off.

"I've got imported Colombian coffee beans, bottles of Dr. Sloane's Horse Liniment, and boxes of Kingsford Starch." Mr. Brewster went around another side of the wagon and pulled things out of nooks and crannies and hidden compartments. The wagon was painted a fiery red with sunny-yellow trim, and the spokes of the wheels were lacquered bright orange.

"A hatbox for traveling, shells for your shotgun, clothesline rope, a jar of udder balm, and the finest twine this side of the Mississippi."

"Zehn," Opa said, looking at me.

"We'll take ten yards of twine, Mr. Brewster," I relayed.

I watched as the huckster measured off the lengths by running the twine from the tip of his nose to the end of his outstretched arm.

"A little extra for good measure," he added, cutting off another length. "Wouldn't want a customer to say they didn't get their money's worth from Les Brewster, now, would we?" He handed me an end, and I began rolling the twine into a ball.

"Neat's-foot oil, sturdy hand brooms, Blatchford's Calf Meal." He looked up, and when he saw we weren't interested, he continued his patter.

"Dyspepsia powders, Dr. Pasteur's Microbe Killer. They say it's good for what ails you. Blue Seal Vaseline, Slippery Elm Lozenges for sore throats, Cooper's Sheep Dip, excellent for lice, ticks, and fleas. Even stops the mange. Dr. Chase's Nerve and Brain Pills, Dr. Barker's Blood Builder." Mr. Brewster was starting to open up another set of doors.

"Dip," Opa said. "Such a big hurry you're in, Mr. Brewster."

Lester Brewster only smiled and handed me the

tin container. He didn't slow down his pace one instant. He even took out his handkerchief and mopped at the beads of perspiration running down the sides of his face. "My, it sure is hot today, isn't it?" he asked me, not really waiting for an answer. All I could think to do was pull my sweater tighter around me to keep out the chilly air.

"Chamber pots, lanterns, pretty calico for the lady of the house. A handsome copper wash boiler. How 'bout some sock stretchers, a sausage grinder, a seed broadcaster—hand-cranked? Real nice. Came in all the way from Indianapolis."

The seed broadcaster caught Opa's attention. Mr. Brewster put his salesmanship into action. I watched as he slipped his arm through the strap and adjusted the bag at his side. Opa and I stared as Mr. Brewster walked over to a bare patch of grass on the side yard and gave us a seed broadcaster demonstration. Flecks of seed sprayed all over the lawn. I saw Opa's face momentarily frown, and he shook his head a little.

"Nein, nein," he mumbled.

"Maybe another time," I told Mr. Brewster, his enthusiasm only flagging for a moment.

"Matches, lamp wicks, new hurricane globes all the way from Pennsylvania," he added. "Got a cousin in Philadelphia, myself," Mr. Brewster volunteered. "Ever been in Philadelphia?"

"Ja," Opa replied, not adding any more.

"That's where his ship landed when he came over to America from the old country," I said. Opa took his cane and swatted me on the back of my legs for having my mouth open when it should have been closed.

"Well, that's a good bit more traveling than I've ever done," Mr. Brewster answered. "I was born and raised in Mishawaka and never left the county till I was eighteen. And look at me now. I took it in my head to become a peddler, and I'm not gonna quit this business till I've been in every county in the state of Indiana. Course, with the sickness going around, business may be a little slow for a while."

"What sickness?" Opa asked.

"Why there's diphtheria going around."

"You mean around here?" I questioned.

"Surely. It's all over Hamilton County. They say two children have died already at the Orphans' Home in Noblesville. Even the undertaker is sick. And it's down the road, too. You can't get much closer than that. I just came from Fanchers' place, and they were putting up the quarantine signs. One of their girls is down with it. The older one."

"Marie Louise?"

"That's it." Mr. Brewster pointed his finger at me. "Marie Louise is the name."

My heart sank. I certainly didn't want anyone at the Fanchers' house to be sick, let alone have diphtheria. I watched Mr. Brewster close up some of the doors and drawers while he kept moving around the wagon. "They think maybe the mother is coming down with it now, too."

Opa frowned at the news.

"A bottle of medicine, we take," he added. "How much do we owe you?"

"Let's see, now. Sheep dip. Twine. Some of that Dr. Pasteur's Microbe Killer. That amounts to forty cents."

Opa took out a small black leather change purse and set the money on the wagon seat.

"Could I trouble you to fill up my water jug?" Mr. Brewster asked, lifting it out from under the front seat. I took it from him and pumped it full of the coldest water I could get. "I've been powerfully thirsty all day today. Hot, thirsty, and tired," he told us.

"Here, little lady, you cut yourself a piece of gum. It's on the house." He showed me a roll of chewing gum hidden behind a door. "And get one for your grandpa, too. The flavors are tutti-frutti or pepsin celery."

I used Opa's penknife and cut us off two slices of tutti-frutti.

"Vielen Dank!" Opa said, staring at the piece.

"Sorry to be in such a hurry, folks, but I'm going
to try and make one more stop today. Thanks for
your business."

He whistled and almost tap-danced a step or two,
jumped up to the wagon, and climbed onto the
seat. We waved as the clinking, clanking wagon
passed through the gate. I marveled one last time at
the shiny yellow paint and the orange spokes. We
stood there chewing on our gum like two old cows
chewing their cud.

"How do you get diphtheria?" I asked Opa.

He kept watching the huckster's wagon as he
spoke to me. "I think it comes from too much dipping."

"Dipping?" I asked, a very puzzled look on my
face.

"Ja, dipping," Opa answered. "Like this." Opa
reached down and planted all ten of his fingers on
my ribs and began tickling me. He tickled and tickled until I almost didn't have any breath left.

"Uncle! Uncle!" I finally remembered to say. I
was in a heap on the ground by then.

Opa gave me a hand up, and we carried the twine
and sheep dip out to the barn.

"Frutti-tutti, frutti-tutti," Opa repeated, practic-
ing the word.

"No, Opa, it's tutti-frutti."

"This chewing gum, I think, it was invented by a cow," Opa offered, moving his jaw like Hester.

"Wouldn't surprise me," I answered, standing by the big doors of the barn.

"Can you spell diphtheria?" Opa asked.

"I don't know," I replied. "I've never thought about it before. D-I-P," I started, but gave up on it. It wasn't too much longer before I found out how it was spelled.

When it was time for bed, Opa made me stand on a chair in the kitchen. I climbed up and stood there in my nightgown as he plaited a four-strand braid down the middle of my back. Before I had time to get down, he was standing in front of me with the bottle of Dr. Pasteur's Microbe Killer.

"I want to see your tonsils," he told me. I aaaah-hhhhed real loud for him, and he spooned in a whole tablespoon full of microbe killer before I knew it.

"Now you don't get the diphtheria," he said, putting the cork back in the top of the bottle.

"Oh no," I said, standing eye to eye with him. "Wait just one minute. You get some, too, you know!"

"Nein," he answered with a frown on his face. "I

am old. No one would care if I get the diphtheria."

"Oh no!" I replied. "What's good for the goose is good for the gander." I took the spoon and bottle out of his hand.

"Aufmachen, bitte!" I ordered.

I suddenly found myself staring into the deep, dark cavern of Opa's mouth.

"Over the lips, past the gums, watch out stomach, here it comes," I recited exactly the same way I'd heard Orin Toliver say it at school. Opa made an awful face.

"Diphtheria won't get us now," I said with authority.

CHAPTER ELEVEN

God Bless Everyone

November of that year stays in my mind so vivid and bold. The rains began the day I put on my long underwear. Countless gray days of drizzle and cold or drenching rains that soaked us clear through to the skin before we could even take cover. Ice puddles covered the paths between the barn and the house. When the rain would let up, the wind would start in and cut right through our coats like a knife.

Opa and I spent most of our evenings in the kitchen not far from the stove and its warmth. Opa worked on harnesses, punching designs into the leather, cutting fringe or braiding fancy strips for halters. He taught me how to do four- and five-strand braids. I practiced them over and over again, making them even and without any twists.

The rest of the month we waited to hear from Katherine.

"Liebe, liebe Katerina," Opa dictated by lamplight one evening.

"English, Opa. We'll have to write Katherine in English," I reminded.

"So how do you like working for a slave driver?" Opa continued, leaning out of the rocker to watch me write. I had placed the piece of paper on my slate board and balanced it on my knees.

"I don't think we can say that, Opa. What if Aunt Mary reads the letter?" I carefully wrote the first few lines. "Dear Katherine," I read, holding up the thin piece of paper, "I miss you something fierce."

"Ja, that is good, but you should write '*We* miss you something fierce,' " Opa corrected. "Ja, much better, that is." I scratched out 'I' and put in a 'we.' "Even Hester misses you," I added. At first I had thought I'd tell her all about school, but there wasn't much to tell. So many children had been sick that Mr. Dreyfus only had us stay until noon each day.

Mostly there was news of the diphtheria outbreak. People stopped visiting or coming around for fear of spreading the sickness. Every Saturday, we waited and hoped for a letter from Katherine, but no letter had arrived in the long, lonely month that she'd been gone. Uncle Mike was our only visitor, our only source of news.

"I heard this morning they've closed the school

down for good," he told us as we sat around the kitchen table dipping thick crusts of bread into bean soup. "Mr. Dreyfus has come down sick, and I heard one of the Pitts boys is sick, too."

"It's not Esco, is it?" I said, looking up. "There are five boys in that family."

"Yes," Uncle Mike confirmed, "that's the one."

"Esco is my friend from school," I told them. "How do you know you've got diphtheria, anyway?" I asked.

"Well, from what I hear, a person gets a powerful sore throat and has a craving for water that won't stop. Then there's the fever."

"Fever? Powerful thirst?"

"Yep, that's right. And a kind of weariness. They say your bones ache."

I looked at Opa. He looked at me.

"The huckster," I said, putting down my spoon. I stood up and went over to Opa's seat and put my hand on his forehead to feel for a fever.

"Ja, the huckster, he was thirsty like you describe, Michael," Opa explained, waving his spoon at Uncle Mike.

"Maybe we're gonna get diphtheria," I told Opa. "Maybe we've already got it, and we don't know it."

"Oh, you'd know it," Uncle Mike reassured me. "You'd be unmercifully sick." He set his bowl in the dry sink and stood by the door, putting on his muffler and hat. A misty rain had started to fall and, every so often, pelts of ice sounded on the parlor window. "They say Orpha Fancher has come down with it real bad."

"So much sad news you have to tell us," Opa replied, pulling on tall boots and mittens. "Here now," Opa said to me, "quick like a bunny, go and get the harness you braided. You can show it to your Uncle Michael."

"Sure," I said, bolting out of the room and running up the stairs two at a time. As I stood on the landing, I heard Uncle Mike talking with Opa.

"How many is this now?" Uncle Mike asked.

"This one makes three," Opa replied.

"What are you gonna do, Johannes, you can't keep ignoring them?"

"Ich weiss nicht," I heard Opa say.

I walked down the steps and saw Opa put something on top of the pie cupboard. I tiptoed back to the stairs and made a lot of noise jumping off the last two or three steps before I went in the kitchen again. Uncle Mike said some very nice things about my braiding and then kissed me on the forehead as he turned to leave.

"Cool as a cucumber," he said with a wink. "No diphtheria hiding in you," he pronounced.

I stood at the kitchen window. He and Opa

walked out to the barn together and pretty soon, Uncle Mike and Blick drove past the house. As soon as I was sure that Opa was in the barn and Uncle Mike was through the gate, I planted one of the kitchen chairs over by the pie cupboard. I was only tall enough to feel with my hands, but I patted the top shelf and felt papers. I grabbed them. When I brought them all down, I found myself holding three letters from Papa.

Using the steam from the teakettle, I worked the flap on one of the envelopes open with a knife. I stood there at the stove with my back to the door and started reading the first letter. I was so intent on Papa's words that I didn't even hear Opa come into the room.

"Was machst du?" he said sharply.

I turned around and held the letter behind my back.

"Nothing," I lied.

"Gib es mir!"

"No!"

"That is not your business," he said, walking toward me.

"This is a letter from my father," I said, waving it in front of me. "How can that not be my business?"

"You are too young."

"Why didn't you tell me about these?" I turned

and picked up the others and held them up. I was nearly shouting. "Three letters! Papa wrote to us and you never even told us."

"Your papa, he did not write to you. He wrote to your mother."

"You're wrong, Opa! These letters are addressed to Katherine and me." I took the latest one Uncle Mike had just brought that day. I ripped open the envelope and read the first few lines.

"This is dated October," I said angrily.

Opa stepped over to me and pulled the letters out of my hands.

"These are not for you to read," he said quickly. He took the letters and put them into his coat pocket. "These mean nothing to you."

"Nothing. They mean everything. They say where Papa is living. They're from Oregon. We know where to find him. Give me the letters," I said, and I tried to get my hand in Opa's pocket.

"Nein," he answered, walking toward the door.

"I want to know where my father is!" I shouted, trying once again to get my hand in Opa's pocket.

With one quick shove, Opa pushed me away and I stumbled into the chair, my cheek catching the edge of the seat as I fell to the floor.

"You can't do this!" I screamed at him.

"I am your opa. I can do what I want," he answered. He stepped up to the stove and opened the firebox. I watched him throw the letters into the middle of the flames.

"I hate you! I hate you!" I said and started to cry.

He turned and walked out to the barn.

I ran into Mama's room and opened up all her dresser drawers. I looked through everything, even the trunk at the foot of the bed for a clue as to where Papa might be. I only found clothes and shoes. There were baby things she'd been making and a packet of letters tied up with a ribbon. I took all these things and sat in the rocker. The letters were from Papa, when they were courting. They were sweet letters, talking about their love for each other and the plans they had. But there was nothing in any of them about Oregon or where Papa was going. I sat there for the longest time with the baby things and letters, and I held them up to my chest and cried and cried. The tears felt cool on my swollen cheek.

Darkness and cold started to come over the house. My stomach was rumbling and I was getting hungry. I went back into the kitchen and stoked up the fire. I lit the kerosene lamp and set it in the middle of the kitchen table.

"I'm never ever gonna say another word to Opa again," I said, taking a single plate down for dinner and placing it on the table. I found one place setting of silver. "I'm never ever gonna turn my hand for him again," I vowed. "How could he do that?" I asked myself over and over. "How could he do that to Katherine and me?" I fixed myself a cup of black tea and sat at the table and set out a slab of bread and potatoes from the back of the warmer on the stove.

I bowed my head and clasped my hands together in prayer. "God in Heaven, bless this food," I said with conviction. "Bless the land and the health of Esco Pitts and Marie Louise and Mrs. Fancher. And bless Harriet and Mr. Fancher. Please don't let anyone else die from diphtheria. God bless Katherine. Bless Papa and bless Mama's soul and my baby brother's soul in Heaven. Dear Lord, even bless Mr. Dreyfus. Bless, bless," I said angrily. "Bless everyone, dear Lord. Bless everyone. Except Opa."

The blackness of evening settled over the house. I looked out toward the barn several times and decided I'd better go and get the milk. Taking the pail of fresh milk to the springhouse was my chore each night. I threw a black cape over my shoulders and put on my bonnet. Opa always set the milk bucket by the door. I knew I could pick up the bucket without even having to say a word to him. The cold night air felt good on my swollen cheek and eye.

But when I creaked open the small door and

stepped inside the barn, the bucket wasn't there. There was a strange silence, then I heard Hester give a plaintive "Moooooo."

"Mooooooo," she bellowed sorrowfully. "Moooooo, Moooooooo."

I ran over to her and found the bucket tipped and milk spilled all over the floor. Cats and kittens were sitting around the damp area, licking their paws and faces. The milking stool was on its side. That's when I caught sight of Opa's leg and saw him lying facedown in Hester's straw bedding.

"Opa!" I called out. I grabbed the sleeve of his jacket, trying to turn him over. With all my might, I pulled on him and managed to get him rolled upon his back. His eyes opened. For a brief second, Opa recognized me.

"Verzeih mir," he whispered. "Verzeih mir."

"I'm sorry, too," I cried. But he closed his eyes again.

"Opa! Opa!" I shouted. "Stay awake." His face was pale white and his lips were bluish. I pounded on his chest to keep him awake, but it didn't seem to do any good. "Oh merciful Father," I said out loud, "what am I gonna do?" I ran out the door, and rain splattered on my face. "Uncle Mike," I called out, but he was long gone. I was almost to the gate. The Fanchers were our nearest neighbors, but I stopped. I couldn't go there. "They're quaran-tined," Uncle Mike's voice said in my mind.

I hurried back into the barn and took hold of Opa's coat. "Wake up, Opa! Wake up!" I shouted. I patted his cheek and searched through his pockets for his nitroglycerine tablets. I finally found the vial in his hand, but when I went to get a pill, the bottle was empty. "I have to get help," I said. I took one of the old blankets we kept in the wagon and covered Opa to try and keep him warm.

"Fanny?" I whispered into the darkness of her stall. She turned to look at me. On tiptoe, I was barely able to reach her bridle and pull it off the nail. I stood by her stall for a long time looking at the bridle in my hand and feeling my heart pound. "Oh, Fanny. Nice horse, gentle horse," I said, step-ping into her stall. "That big, loud thumping sound is only my heart, Fanny. Don't let it scare you."

I knew there was nothing else I could do. Doc Taylor's house was seven miles away.

CHAPTER TWELVE

Steady, Girl, Steady

"Whoa, girl," I coaxed. Fanny whinnied and sidestepped as I walked up to her with the bridle. I climbed up the sides of the stall and hooked one leg through the railing. Fanny was a beauty of a Morgan. I was lucky she was only fourteen hands high. I was lucky, too, she was good in the harness and good in the saddle. Opa always liked to have Morgans, and Fanny was a sweetheart of a horse.

"Easy girl." My hands were shaking so badly I could barely slip the bit into her mouth and pull the bridle over her ears. The reins hung down to the straw. "That was easy, now, wasn't it?" I said, more for me than her. My legs were so wobbly I could hardly stand when my feet landed on the soft straw of the barn floor.

I hurried over to open one of the big barn doors.

"Don't worry, Fanny, we're gonna do fine," I told her as I walked beside her. I put my trembling hand on her flank, and she turned to look at me with her big brown eyes. "We're gonna go for a little ride," I said, talking to her the way Opa always did. I reached down to grab the reins, and she nibbled at my sleeve.

I walked Fanny outside and stood beside her in the icy rain.

We started down the lane and for a few seconds I was so frightened I almost thought about walking all the way to Doc Taylor's. But with the darkness and the cold, I knew I'd never make it.

"Over here, girl," I said. I walked her near one of the gates leading out to a cornfield. Fanny was watching my every move. She held her head high and her ears were perked up. She must've sensed how scared I was.

"Whoa, girl, whoa. Whoa," I tried to say with authority. I put my hand on her shoulder to keep her steady. I took a deep breath, pulled my skirts to one side, and climbed onto the top rail of the fence.

"Steady, girl, steady," I begged. When she was very, very still, I held onto the fence post to balance myself and slipped one leg over her back.

"Whoa, whoa. Easy, easy," I said. She stepped away from the fence and put her head down to munch on the grass.

"No, no, Fanny, don't do that. We've got to go into town."

I could tell she didn't like it when I kept her head up so she couldn't munch, but I knew if we walked, I'd be reining her up every few yards.

I took the reins and wrapped them around my left wrist. I took my fingers and grabbed two handfuls of her mane down at her withers. I tried to hold as tight as I could without hurting her. The rain pelted my face like sharp little needles. I started to cry. I put my head down close enough to Fanny's neck to feel the warmth of her skin. Then with absolute fear in my heart and my stomach up in my throat, I said, "Giddyup!" I dug my heels good and hard into her sides.

Fanny took off like a shot.

"It's all right now, honey, you can let go," Mrs. Taylor said as Doc tried to help me down. My hands were clenched so tight, they wouldn't let go of Fanny's mane.

Doc gently worked his fingers under mine, and I slid off Fanny into his arms.

"It's Opa, it's Opa," I kept saying over and over. "He's in the barn. He won't wake up. Something's happened to him. His pills are gone. Please help us."

Doc nodded. He tried to get me to stand, but my legs wouldn't hold me.

"Here, Julianna," he said to his wife, "take her inside. Get her some dry things while I hitch up the buggy."

Mrs. Taylor propped me up in a chair and hung a change of clothes to warm by the stove. She peeled the rain-soaked cape off my arms and helped me out of my dress. She toweled my hair and rubbed my legs with warm washcloths until the feeling started to come back in them. The toasty clothes felt good as I put them on.

We heard the buggy pull up in front of the house. Doc Taylor came in, still in his shirtsleeves. "I only need to get my coat and my bag, then we can leave." Mrs. Taylor bundled me up and I sat next to Doc in the covered buggy. The rain had stopped and the stars were coming out from behind wispy clouds. The air was crisp and cold, and I could see our breath each time we spoke. Doc had tied Fanny to the back of the buggy. He'd thrown a blanket over her to keep her from getting chilled.

Doc put smelling salts under Opa's nose to revive him. Between the two of us we were able to get him from the barn to the house. I went in and stoked up the fire and put a big pan of water for boiling instruments on the stove. I stood by Opa's bed while

Doc checked him over. Doc listened with the stethoscope to Opa's heart and looked in his eyes. Doc tapped on Opa's knees with a mallet and even took his temperature. I looked away when Doc gave Opa a shot with a great big hypodermic needle. Opa tried to speak.

"My ticker," Opa said hoarsely, "is not tocking so good. Ja, Herr Doktor?"

"That's right, Mr. Kreuzer. You take it easy. I want you to do absolutely nothing for the next few days. You're very fortunate. You've had a very bad spell with your heart. What you need to do now is simply stay put in this bed. You and your heart should have complete rest. I don't want you getting out of bed for at least a month."

For once, Opa looked too tired to even argue. He nodded his head and closed his eyes. Doc motioned for me to follow him, and we went into the kitchen.

"Your grandfather's had a heart attack, Callie. He's going to need absolute quiet and complete bedrest for the next few weeks." Doc set his medical bag on the kitchen table and took out a bottle filled with little white pills. He poured two or three dozen into a paper envelope and wrote "Johannes Kreuzer" across the front. "These are more heart pills," he explained. "You know that one goes . . ." he started to say, but I finished, "under his tongue."

"Exactly." Doc sighed. He put his hand on my head. "You've had quite a day, haven't you, sweetie?"

"Yes sir, I guess I have."

"You sit yourself down here a minute, and I'll take a look at you next."

I aaaaaahhhed for Doc, and he took my temperature. He looked in my ears.

"No potatoes in there," he said with a laugh. Then he touched the bruise on my face.

"What a shiner! How'd this happen?" he asked.

"I fell off the horse," I lied, remembering how it stung when my face hit the side of the chair.

"You'll have a first-class black eye out of it," he explained. "Otherwise, you're no worse for the wear." He closed up his bag and put on his coat. "You know, Callie, you did a brave thing, riding to my house the way you did."

"Yes sir," was the only thing I could think to say.

"Don't forget to check Fanny. Make sure she's cooled down and has hay and water. I'll stop by tomorrow, if I'm out this way," he said. "And you, little lady, you keep nice and warm tonight. Make sure your grandfather has plenty of rest and lots of liquids. Give him anything he wants to eat to help build up his strength. He's not gonna look much like himself for a while." Doc tousled my hair and patted me on the shoulder.

"Thank you for everything, Doc."

"That's what I'm here for. Better find the bottle of horse liniment."

"It's in the barn by Fanny's stall."

"Well, bring it in the house."

"In the house?"

"Yep, you're gonna need it. Come morning you're gonna be stiff as a board."

By lamplight, Fanny's bright eyes looked bigger than ever.

"Hello there," I said, holding up the lantern. I hung it on a nail by her stall and grabbed an armful of fresh hay for her. I put my hand under her blanket and felt along her loin. She was warm and dry.

"We did it, you know," I told her. I stood next to her and rested my head on her neck. "Thank you, Fanny," I said softly. She turned to nibble at my hair. I ran my fingers down the smooth, velvety part of her nose and gave her a kiss on the muzzle. "Good night, you sweet four-legged thing." I patted her once more.

"We did it," I said as I pulled the lantern off the

nail and walked out of the barn. "By golly, we did it."

Walking across the yard, I looked up at the clear night sky.

"I hope you saw me, Katherine," I shouted to the top star of Orion's Belt. "I would've made you proud!"

I checked on Opa one last time. Standing beside the bed and holding the lantern high, I could see his chest rise and fall under the covers. He was sleeping soundly and didn't even stir when I touched his shoulder.

After I added another log to the stove, I draped blankets over the rocker and pulled it closer to the heat. I poured myself a mug of cocoa. I kept a cool washcloth on my eye and soaked my feet in warm Epsom salts water for a little while. I rubbed horse liniment on my calves and arms.

"Peee-uuuuu," I said from the smell. I curled up all toasty warm into the blankets and fixed a pillow under my head. I nested myself into the rocker like an old hen so that I could hear Opa if he called out.

The clock striking twelve woke me up and the eerie light from the kerosene lamp played tricks on my eyes. I thought I saw Mama standing in the shadows by the dry sink.

"Mama, is that you?" I whispered, but the minute

my words broke the silence of the house, I knew I had only imagined the whole thing. A log shifted in the fire, and I pulled the blankets up higher around my shoulders. I closed my eyes, and I could almost see Mama standing at the kitchen table working, her skirts gently rustling. She always sang when she worked. I knew for certain which hymn she'd be singing, and I sang it faintly.

"Softly and tenderly, Jesus is calling." My voice sounded tiny and thin. "Calling for you and for me."

It was one of Mama's favorite hymns. I'd heard her sing it again and again, right there while she worked in the kitchen.

"See on the portals He's waiting and watching, watching for you and for me."

I thought of Opa and the cold evening and how empty the house felt without Mama and Katherine and Papa. It felt good to sing to Jesus that night and my tiny voice grew stronger. My mind nearly tricked me into believing I heard Mama singing along with me.

"Come home, come home. Ye who are weary, come home, come home. Earnestly, tenderly, Jesus is calling. Calling, O Sinner, come home."

In the end, as I sat in the darkness and the quiet of our kitchen, it was my voice that was singing all by itself. Quiet but strong just the same. As much as I wanted it to be me and Mama singing, I knew deep down in my heart, it was only me.

"Mama," I heard myself say out loud, "Mama, I miss you so much. You're really gone, aren't you?" And the clock ticking in the parlor and the creaking of our motherless house was my answer.

CHAPTER THIRTEEN

Fanchers' Farm

The flat, gray light of morning came in the window and pried my eyes open. The fire was cold, and all the kerosene was burned out of the lamp.

"Oh mercy," I moaned, as I tried to move. Every bone in my body ached. The crick in my neck was so bad that I could barely turn my head. I wrestled myself free of the blankets and went into the bedroom to check on Opa.

His loud snoring was music to my ears.

My fingers pained me so much that striking a match to start the fire was almost impossible. I stood by the kitchen window and watched a hot pink color wash across the sky in the east.

While I was frying strips of bacon, I heard a wagon pull into the yard. I ran to the door to see Uncle Mike hurrying along the path.

"Doc Taylor got word to me last night," Uncle Mike said. He came in and held his hat in his hands.

"How is he?" he asked. "And how are you?" he said, putting his hand on my shoulder. "Doc said you rode all seven miles bareback on Fanny." Uncle Mike touched my cheek. I winced a bit.

"Oooooooheeeeeh," he exclaimed. "Looks like you connected with the wrong end of a horse!"

"Opa's still asleep," I told him, rubbing my elbows and pulling up my shoulders. "I'm stiff as a board, but I'm gonna be fine."

Uncle Mike and I went in together to see Opa. As we stood there whispering, Opa awoke and held out his hand to both of us.

"I'll make you some tea," I told him, and Opa seemed grateful.

Having Uncle Mike there was a blessing. He helped me with Opa. We propped him up in bed with every pillow in the house. Together we helped feed him a little tea and toast and took our plates of fried eggs and potatoes and bacon into the bedroom so we could keep him company.

While Uncle Mike chopped kindling, I milked Hester.

She was mooing and mooing by the time I got out there, glad as anything for the relief.

"Meine gute, schöne Kuh," I said to her the way Opa did every morning and evening when he milked her. I squirted milk to a row of cats and kittens. They carefully cleaned their paws and faces after I'd caught them in the head or on the back with a stream of milk. I gave Fanny more hay and turned her out into the back pasture. She kicked up her heels to be out of the barn for a while on such a beautiful day. The sun shone so brightly that the ice puddles began melting.

Opa slept the rest of the morning and well into the afternoon. Not long after lunch, I was sitting at the kitchen table. I put my head down on my arms and fell sound asleep. Loud knocks came from our front door and woke me up.

"Mr. Fancher," I said as I pulled the door open.

"Keep your distance, Callie," he said quickly. He pulled his hat off his head. "We're still in quarantine, and I probably shouldn't even be here."

"Orville," Uncle Mike said, standing beside me, "what can we do for you?"

Mr. Fancher turned his face away from us and looked off into the distance. It was a long time before he spoke.

"I've come by," he started to say and stopped to clear his throat. "I've come by to say that," he cleared his throat again, "my Orpha passed away early this morning." He took a hankie out of his pants pocket and covered his mouth.

When Uncle Mike started to speak, Mr. Fancher motioned with his hand as though he had more to say. "We're gonna bury her in the morning up at our place. You bein' neighbors and all, we just wanted you to know."

"Orville," Uncle Mike said, stepping closer to the door, "we're so sorry to hear your news." Mr. Fancher stood on the porch and turned his face away from us. It seemed as though it was hard for him to look at us, but it also seemed as though he didn't want to leave.

"Is Marie Louise any better?" I asked.

"She's holding her own, Callie. Seems like she's come through the worst of it. But with her mother passing away . . ." Then Mr. Fancher didn't seem able to go on.

Uncle Mike nodded his head. "She's young, Orville," Uncle Mike said, trying to give Mr. Fancher a ray of hope. Mr. Fancher looked out toward his wagon.

"I'd better be goin'," he told us.

"Orville," Uncle Mike said quickly, "I'll follow you back this afternoon." Uncle Mike held up his hand as Mr. Fancher tried to tell him not to come, but Uncle Mike insisted.

"I'll come over and do your milking tonight," he said. He turned to go into the kitchen to put on his hat and coat.

"Mr. Fancher," I asked, "will you tell Harriet I asked about her, please?"

"Thank you, Callie," he answered. "Yes, I will.

She's had a bad time of it, what with her mother passing away and Marie Louise so sick. We're both plum wore out."

As Uncle Mike and Mr. Fancher went down our lane, I ran up the steps to the attic and looked out, directly to the west. I could barely make out Fanchers' place in the growing twilight with its one tree and house and barn. Their farm stood out on a stretch of flat farmland like an oasis. More than anything, though, what I could see in my mind was a picture of Mrs. Fancher at the threshing dinner. She was smiling and coming out of our kitchen door, holding that big pan full of fried chicken with both hands.

Uncle Mike stayed the night. The next morning, I bundled up good and tight to go to Fanchers' for the funeral. I baked them a loaf of buttermilk bread, and I was glad to keep it on my lap for the warmth. There was only Pastor Greene's buggy and ours in the yard. Big, bold QUARANTINE—DIPHTHERIA signs tried to warn us away. I never again wondered how to spell the word. A black wreath had been hung on the door, and we stood with Pastor Greene on the porch. No one inside came out and not a soul outside went in.

"I'm glad you could come," Pastor Greene said as

we shook gloved hands. The sermon was short and he spoke a jumble of words I don't remember since it was biting cold. My knees were knocking together. Uncle Mike moved me in front of him so his body could break the wind.

Our three small voices sang two hymns carried away by the gusting wind. At the appointed time, Pastor Greene directed us to pay our respects and file past the front window that looked into the Fanchers' living room. There, in front of the big parlor window, was Mrs. Fancher, laid out in her coffin. Her color was a yellowish white and her cheeks were nearly sunk down to her teeth. Her hands looked like bones covered with gauze. The ruffles on the bodice of her dress seemed to be the part that made up her chest. Of course, she wasn't the first dead person I'd ever seen. That part didn't scare me much. But what scared me was to see Marie Louise.

Mr. Fancher and Harriet were standing together near the window. Marie Louise was seated in a chair beside her mother's coffin. A blanket was draped around her shoulders and an afghan stretched across her lap. The way she sat there in a trance, I thought Marie Louise really and truly looked as dead as her mother. The skin on her face seemed like it had been stretched across the bones of her cheeks. Her blond hair was stringy and brownish in color and flattened to her skull. She never once looked away from her mother's coffin. Marie Louise never once moved. It was all I could do not to stare at her.

As we stood in front of the window, I leaned up against the house and touched the glass with my hand. Harriet moved and I nearly jumped away, but she walked over and put her hand onto the glass as if to touch mine. For a brief moment, I felt the warmth come through. I looked at her and saw her eyes filled with tears, spilling over and running down her cheeks.

We stood there in the bitter cold. Pastor Greene sang "Abide With Me," and then a chilling wind started to grab at my legs and arms.

Pastor Greene and Uncle Mike went around the side of the house. I heard the unmistakable sound of wood splintering and glass shattering. I stood on the end of the Fanchers' porch and watched as Mr. Fancher handed things out to Pastor Greene and Uncle Mike. They had both put on gloves and tied kerchiefs across their noses and mouths like bank robbers. Piece by piece, they began emptying the furniture out of the room through the window. A rug, a chair, a washstand, the frame of a dresser, the individual drawers. Their contents were spilled out onto the lawn. Dresses were strewn over the pile of things. Even the pictures off the walls perched precariously amongst the items. Curtains, bedding, and blankets. The men heaped everything onto the pile until nothing remained in the room, not even Mrs. Fancher's new wicker sewing basket.

Pastor Greene sloshed kerosene all over the mound of things. He struck a handful of matches and threw them onto the pile. The sewing basket exploded into flames, crackling and popping as it caught on fire. Then the orange flames licked their way onto the nightstand and dresser. In only a few seconds, yellow flames engulfed everything. Inky black smoke billowed up into the sky. I stood there with the heat on one side of me, a freezing rain sprinkling down my neck, and a chill in my heart. Both men took off their gloves and kerchiefs and threw them into the flames.

I left the loaf of bread on the porch by the front door. As Uncle Mike and I turned to get into the wagon, I sneaked one more look at the house. Harriet came outside and waved. She held the loaf of bread in her arm. Inside, Marie Louise was still propped up in the same chair, staring at the coffin and her dead mother.

We pulled away from the house and I thought about our two farms. How they felt so lost and alone, surrounded now by empty fields. How we were both without mothers.

"Why is it mothers have to die?" I asked Uncle

Mike, but he never answered me. I stared at Uncle Mike's bare hands and saw how worn and calloused they were as he held Fanny's reins. I certainly didn't have an answer. The thought struck me that maybe Uncle Mike didn't have an answer either.

I glanced over my shoulder as we turned onto Mule Barn Road. I watched the thick black smoke from the fire billow into the graying sky. Even by the time we got to the top of Hollyhock Hill, the smoke was still curling up into the dark, November clouds. It looked as though the oasis of Fanchers' farm would burn itself right off the face of the horizon line.

CHAPTER FOURTEEN

A Thousand Candles

Our first letter from Katherine came the following week. Uncle Mike was out visiting, and he'd brought us the mail.

Her letter was very short. Opa frowned the entire time I read him her note.

"Dear Opa and Callie," I read from the thin sheet of paper. "I am sending you my first pay from working for Aunt Mary. I hope to come home for a visit on Christmas. Love, Katherine."

"That is all?" Opa asked.

"Yes," I replied. "Nothing more. She sent money."

"Money?" he asked. "And how much has she sent?"

I stared at the money wrapped in a single piece of paper. I knew Katherine had been gone for well over a month, more like two months. I also remembered how Aunt Mary had boasted that Katherine would make a great deal of money, even more than the fifteen or eighteen dollars she'd get teaching school.

Carefully and slowly, I counted the dollar bills and coins.

"Nine dollars and thirty-seven cents," I answered Opa.

"That is all?" Opa asked again. "Are you sure?"

I counted the money one more time. "Nine dollars and thirty-seven cents," I repeated.

Opa threw back the bedcovers and hung his lily-white legs over the side of the bed.

"Where are you goin'? You're not supposed to get out of bed for a month," I said, trying to sound like Doc Taylor.

"My Katerina, she is working for a driver of slaves," he answered.

I knew Opa was still very wobbly on his feet. He clung to the sides of the mattress, not even trying to stand. I hesitated a few seconds before I answered.

"That's very true, Opa," I admitted, "but I think you're going to need all your strength before you go and bring her back home. I don't think you're strong enough yet."

"I can bring her home, Johannes," Uncle Mike offered. "I can make the trip to Noblesville and bring her out here on Christmas Day."

Opa didn't answer. He only stared at his feet as they dangled over the side of the bed.

"Nine dollars and thirty-seven cents," he repeated. "A driver of slaves that Mary is," he muttered. "Such a miser. She pinches pennies so hard they squeal." His head sagged. I helped him put his feet back under the covers and I tucked the blankets in under his chin again. "Ja, Michael, you bring her home," Opa said. "By Christmas, I will be my old self again."

"That's fine with me, Opa," I told him honestly. I missed Katherine ferociously and wanted her home more than he probably knew.

"Only nine dollars and thirty-seven cents," he muttered, shaking his head. "Schrecklich! Schrecklich!"

In the evenings, Opa and I played checkers, or after one of Uncle Mike's visits, I would read to Opa. On the Saturdays Uncle Mike brought us a paper, I always sat in a chair beside Opa's bed reading to him while he ate his lunch on a tray. We had a little game we played, and we both knew the rules. First Opa took the paper and went through it, pretending to read it over the tops of his glasses. He'd make big sweeping motions turning the pages and spend a lot of time poring over the pictures.

Then he'd say, "Almost the English I can read," as he handed me the sections. "A little better it is this week," and he'd point to a headline or an ad for something.

"Where would you like for me to start?" I always asked.

"First, the weather. There," Opa said, pointing to a small column at the top near the headline. Uncle Mike brought us papers that were always several days late.

"The weather," I read. "Fair and warmer tonight. Cloudy by Tuesday."

"What the day is today?" Opa always asked.

"Sunday," I answered.

Opa would scratch his chin and tap his fingers on his cheek. "Tuesday, Tuesday. A little I am thinking on this," then he'd gaze off for a few seconds. "Dienstag, Dienstag. Ja, der Himmel war bewölkt. Yes. It most certainly was cloudy last Tuesday."

On the Saturday that Uncle Mike brought the letter from Katherine, I was reading the headlines to Opa, the same way Mama always had at lunchtime.

"Senator Bailey replies to Mr. Bryan's speech." I knew to look up to see whether Opa wanted me to go on.

"Nein," Opa replied.

"Governor Johnson reported dying."

"Nein."

"Taft reopens railroad war."

"This Taft President," Opa said, but changed his mind and waved me on to another headline.

"Cook to reach U.S. tomorrow."

"We have plenty cooks in United States," Opa said with a puzzled look on his face. "What do we need more cooks for?" he asked.

"This here says it's Dr. Frederick A. Cook, Polar Explorer."

"Nein, no cooks today."

"Chicago prices for milk."

"Read," Opa commanded with a frown. He loved to hear the farm news.

"Chicago, November tenth. The Milk Producers' Association, controlling sixty-five percent of the milk shipped to Chicago, threatens to establish retail depots unless the big milk companies agree to an advanced sale."

Opa leaned back and closed his eyes. I knew to move on to the grocery columns, but the more I read, the more my eyes drooped. My arms were so tired I could barely hold up the paper. I'd been getting up at 5:30 A.M. to milk Fanny, and mornings were spent with cooking and washing. By afternoon, I needed a nap, just like a baby. Most evenings, I could barely keep my eyes open.

"Wright Brothers Grocery is selling butter for

twenty-nine cents a pound. Three cans of salmon for twenty-five cents. Three cans of Campbell's Soup for a quarter and five pounds of sugar for six cents," I read from the last page. "Your backache will yield to Lydia E. Pinkham's vegetable compound."

"What needs fixing is not my back," Opa said, opening his eyes. "See if there is an ad for a new heart, Herzchen," he joked. When he turned to look at me, I was nearly asleep sitting up.

"Herzchen, Herzchen," Opa said, leaning over and tapping me on the knee.

"My little Florence Nightingale, she is exhausted, ja? All this nursing of your Opa, it makes you tired."

"Ja, Opa," I replied with a yawn.

"Here," Opa motioned. He scooted over so I could nestle into his arm. I spread the afghan over my legs, and the minute my head rested on Opa's chest, I was fast asleep. Little did I know that within a few weeks' time I'd really know what it was like to be a bone-tired nurse.

While Opa was recovering, I learned to cook. He was brave to try all the things I made. Because we had so little money and our supplies were low, we even had to eat my mistakes and the burned things. Dinners were usually "Himmel und Erde," as Opa called it. Heaven and Earth in English, or apples and potatoes cooked together. Once in a while we'd have beans and corn bread. Or maybe as a treat, I'd make us a little "Schnitz und Knopfen," what we called apples and buttons, which amounted to dried apples with slices of sausage. Every Wednesday I rolled out long, flat sheets of noodle dough. I cut long thin strips and let them dry, hanging over a broom handle suspended between two chairs. I learned what it takes to make bread rise, too. That winter, my specialty was baking bread that would've seen better use as bricks for a chimney than for eating.

On a mild December day, I made soap. While I built up the fire under the big black kettle, Opa brought out a chair and supervised. It was his first time outside since the bad spell with his heart. I brought out the cans of pork rinds we'd saved and stored in the smokehouse. I gingerly carried over the lye bucket. Rainwater that came off the roof of the smokehouse ran through a barrel of stove ashes. This made the lye we needed for soapmaking.

Mama had been the soapmaker in the family. She liked to sing "The Crusader's Hymn" when she worked outside. I stood by the kettle of boiling rainwater, listening to it bubble and pop. Without even thinking, I began singing. I let the song come straight out of my heart and into the open air. "Beautiful Saviour, ruler of all creation."

"Such a nice voice you have, Callie," Opa told me when I was done.

I added the cubes of pork lard and drippings. I carefully poured in the lye. As the hunks of pork fat began to melt, the mixture smelled strangely of a roast pork dinner. I slowly stirred the contents of the kettle with an old hickory ax handle. The front of me facing the fire warmed up toasty hot while my backside stayed cool. But a question was boiling up inside of me. Once everything in the pot started to bubble up good, I found myself humming the second verse. Opa joined me with the harmony. "Fairer are the meadows. Fairer still the woodlands. Robed in the flowers of the blooming spring." We sang to the silent cornfields.

I added a few pieces of wood to the fire, standing close by and stirring to make sure the soap didn't spew over the sides of the pot.

"Opa?" I asked, trying to keep an eye on the kettle but watching him at the same time. "Why didn't you let us see Papa's letters? Why did you hide them?"

Opa was sitting with one leg crossed over the other, his elbows resting on his knees.

"A bad decision I made," he answered. "I could

not read your letters because I cannot read the English," he said. He stood up and came over to me.
"And I was afraid of what they might say." We both
stared into the kettle.

"I was afraid your papa would send for you." He
put his arm around me and held me tight. "I am an
old man, and it is a simple thing. You are everything to me. You and Katherine are all I have now.
I was afraid to find out that your papa would come
home. That he would take you away from me."

"You mean to Oregon?"

"Ja, all the way to Oregon."

"But, Opa, you can come, too. I just know you
can."

"Maybe your papa, he says no. Then again,
maybe I don't want to come along. Such an old man
I am. Your papa and I, we don't get along so well.
Perhaps I am better off to stay here."

"Opa, that's silly. You could come out to Oregon
with us. Why, it's beautiful there. Oregon is so lush
and green."

"Now you are sounding like your father."

"I want you to come with us, Opa. Please think
about it."

"A little I will think on this."

I let the soap cook itself down and thicken up to
the right consistency. When I dipped the ax handle
into the middle of the pot and pulled it straight up,

soap dripped off the end of the handle and stranded in a thick thread that twirled into a circle. I did this two or three times before the thread suited Opa. We were ready to pour the soap into a tub to harden.

"Wait," I said and ran over to the back porch. I found the bottle Mama kept on the shelf. "Mama always put some of this in the soap so it would smell nice," I told him. I poured in a little sassafras oil and gave it a stir.

Opa and I ladled out the soap. I took a long stick and broke up the fire under the kettle. Together, we carried the tub over to the porch to let it cool down. A small dried leaf blew onto the top and stuck. It looked pretty lying there, flattened out. I left it in the soap. Later that night, we would take a long corn knife and cut the nearly hardened soap into blocks.

Several weeks passed by, and long about twilight, Harriet Fancher rode into the yard on her pony, Taffy.

"It's me, Harriet," she said as though she was afraid I might not remember her. "We're out of quarantine," she explained with a smile, but I couldn't get her to come into the kitchen.

"We want you and your grandfather to come

over," she said. "It's for Marie Louise," then she added, "well, it's going to be for Christmas Eve. Doc said he thought it might do her good."

"Christmas Eve is soon?" I asked, realizing one day had simply melted into another.

"Yes," she answered. "Can you be there for dinner?"

"We'll be there," Opa said for both of us. "Mit Glöckchen," he added.

"With bells on," I said, smiling and laughing all at once.

"Oh, that's wonderful," Harriet said, seeming truly grateful. "I'm so glad."

"What should we bring?" Opa asked.

"Just bring yourselves," Harriet replied. "To come to our house, you only need to bring yourselves."

That night the wind turned cold and chilling. When I went out to check on Fanny and Hester, the sky was spitting snow. By the time I came back in, Opa had moved a cot into the kitchen for me. We made up my bed near the stove. He sat in the rocker, and I burrowed under a mound of covers. Every once in a while, I'd see the bowl of his pipe glow all orangey whenever he took a puff. I watched as he blew smoke rings for me up into the air.

"Opa, I almost forgot about Christmas," I told him.

"Christmas I had not forgotten, mein Herzchen. Without your mother, I was trying not to let myself think about it, I suppose."

"Do they have Christmas in Heaven?"

I listened to Opa rock back and forth a few times, then go back and forth a few more times before he answered.

"Ja, in Heaven they have Christmas," he answered softly. "In Heaven, I believe there is an enormous Tannenbaum. A Christmas tree so lovely, it is covered with beautiful candles. Eintausend Kerzen."

"That many, Opa? A thousand candles?"

"Ja, eintausend Kerzen. And the Christ child is in his cradle. Your oma and your mama and your baby brother and your uncle Erich, they are there, too."

"What are they all doing?"

Lying there in the fading glow of the kerosene lamp, I thought maybe Opa hadn't heard me, so I asked again.

"What are they all doing, Opa? Do you think they're lonely? I wonder sometimes if Mama is lonely. I wonder if she misses me, the way I miss her. I didn't even get to say good-bye to her, Opa."

"A little I am thinking on this, Herzchen," he replied, puffing out a set of smoke rings.

"Your mama is not lonely, Herzchen. Of this, I am sure. From Heaven she watches over you every day. You bring her joy, even in Heaven. And she has your oma and Uncle Erich to keep her company."

"I'm glad she's not lonely," I whispered to Opa. "I couldn't bear the thought of Mama being up there in Heaven and being lonely," I told him.

"Ja," he replied. "Knowing she is with Jesus and your oma and your baby brother and Uncle Erich is the only thing that makes her being gone a little easier to bear."

The rocking chair scraped on the bare floorboards as Opa scooted it closer to the cot. I reached out and put his big gnarled hand in mine. I closed my eyes and listened to the crackling of the fire and the steady thumping of the rocker. All the while, I was thinking of Oma, Uncle Erich, and Mama holding the baby. The three of them standing together admiring a giant Christmas tree. An enormous Christmas tree with a thousand sparkling candles, right in the middle of Heaven.

CHAPTER FIFTEEN

My Sister, Katherine

"A very Merry Christmas to you, Johannes, and to you, Callie," Mr. Fancher said when he greeted us at the door. I always loved to go to the Fanchers' since their house was so different from ours. For one thing, it always smelled of cinnamon and spices. The Fanchers were worldly enough to have a Christmas tree, and this Christmas Eve was no different from any other. Harriet came out of the kitchen and greeted us, wearing her mother's long cooking apron.

"Where's Marie Louise?" I asked. Harriet pointed to a chair in the parlor that faced a window.

"She's still poorly, and we thought maybe having you over to celebrate Christmas might help," Harriet explained. "Doc says to try and draw her back into our world, gradual. He thinks maybe, in time, she'll get over Mama's death."

"We brought you a little something," I said, holding out a small package wrapped in brown paper.

"Oh, Callie, this is lovely," Harriet said, admiring the leaf. She walked over to her sister. "Marie Louise, look what Callie brought for us. It's a bar of soap." She stopped to sniff it. "It smells of sassafras. It's a wonderful present, Callie."

Marie Louise turned to look at her father with empty eyes. When I stepped into her line of vision, she looked at me as if I were a stranger.

"It's me, Marie Louise. It's Callie Common," I said and took hold of Marie Louise's hand. I was surprised at how warm and smooth it was.

"Callie?" she asked, not even looking at me. "It's nice you could come."

Marie Louise sat quiet as a mouse. As I was turning to walk away, she said something that made a chill run up my back.

"Mama will be with us in a few minutes. She'll be out here to say hello, herself. She always liked you, Callie."

While Opa and Mr. Fancher talked in the parlor, I helped Harriet finish everything in the kitchen. My mouth began to water just looking at the food Harriet and her father had made for all of us. A pot of potatoes bubbled on the back of the stove and a stuffed capon waited on a platter on the warming shelf.

"I never can get biscuits right," Harriet said impatiently. "They're either raw inside, or hard as a rock."

"It's too bad Katherine's not here," I told Harriet. "But she's coming home tomorrow," I explained.

"You must be so glad."

"Yes, I never thought I'd miss my sister so much."

"I'm glad the quarantine is over," Harriet told me. "It's been powerful lonely here. Papa's tried so hard. And Marie Louise, well, it's almost like she isn't here anymore."

"Does she still believe your mama is alive?"

"Some days she does. Other days she doesn't. Doc wants us to try and keep the days Marie Louise believes Mama is dead, outnumbering the days she doesn't."

I handed Harriet a dish towel.

"Oh mercy," she said. She fumbled with the towel, wadding it up to pull out a tray of biscuits, unquestionably burned to a crisp.

"This is the second batch I ruined. Pa's gonna be perturbed with me for sure."

"Make another batch. Here, I'll help you." I took the pan from her and dumped the biscuits into my apron. "I've seen Katherine do this more times than I can count. Come on."

We stood on the steps of the back porch.

"Here, Jack. Here, King. Here, Red," we called. The coonhounds Mr. Fancher used for hunting came right over, their tails wagging. They sniffed at my apron. Harriet and I each took a handful of hard, round biscuits and threw them with our pitching arms as far out into the yard as we could. The dogs chased after those biscuits, leaping and cavorting, snarling with each other over every little morsel.

"See, Harriet," I laughed, "they like your biscuits just fine."

"They'd eat anything," she answered and threw another biscuit high into the air. Snowflakes landed on our faces and eyelashes as we stood there. The last of the biscuits bounced along the ground and the dogs jumped after them. Before long, every crumb of evidence had disappeared.

In no time at all, Harriet had mixed the lard, flour, and salt together for another batch. She slid a fresh trayful of biscuits into the oven. I helped her set the table and brought out a pitcher of buttermilk. We made a pot of coffee for the men and finally called everyone in to eat.

We passed the sausage stuffing and mashed potatoes twice. I managed to eat a drumstick and thigh all by myself. The food tasted so good. It was such a pleasure to share a meal with other folks that day. Harriet and I listened as Opa and Mr. Fancher talked about crops and animals and spring planting.

"Will Weaver's gonna try soybeans down on his place come this spring."

"Ja, soybeans?" Opa answered between mouthfuls of mashed potatoes.

"Yep, says he'll get twenty bushels an acre."

"Ja, really? That is very good. I would say extraordinary."

"Yep, but those soybeans, they're too exotic for me," Mr. Fancher continued. "Corn's what I like to grow. Maybe I'll sow that front pasture out by the road into rye grass a little earlier this spring. I got that in awful late last year." And the talk went on and on. The two men seemed as lonely for the company as we were. They talked about calving and milk prices while they drank their coffee.

Only once did Marie Louise act strangely. We were passing out plates of BobAndy pie when she suddenly broke her long silence.

"Where's Mama's place?" she asked. "There's no place set for Mama?"

Mr. Fancher looked from me to Opa, then back to Marie Louise again.

"She won't be here today for dinner, Marie Louise," he explained. Marie Louise seemed to take him at his word and not want more of an answer. But it still gave me the chills the way she kept talking about Mrs. Fancher as though she were alive.

"You girls were generous enough to cook so I'll do the cleanup," Mr. Fancher offered.

"Nein," Opa contradicted. "*We* will do the clean-up," he corrected.

Harriet and I tied our aprons around the waists of the two men. We found ourselves pieces of clean string and sat by the kitchen stove playing string games. We twisted and twirled out cat's cradles, cup 'n' saucers, and witches' broomsticks to stay occupied.

"Seein' as how it's a holiday and all," Mr. Fancher told Harriet, "why don't you get out the picture cards? As long as you treat them gingerly," he said kindly.

Harriet and I sat on the sofa and traded looks at the stereoscope. We carefully put in a new card and read each caption in awe.

"Will you look at all that money?" I said as I passed over the viewer with a card showing a table holding one million six hundred thousand dollars piled on top of it. The people and places looked so real, it seemed like we could almost reach right out and touch them.

In a matter of seconds, we could go from pictures of Cheyenne, Wyoming, in the Old West to two people standing in front of the great Matterhorn mountain in Switzerland.

"This here picture shows the 'Colossal Iron Statue of Vulcan,'" Harriet read from the card. "It's at the World's Fair in St. Louis."

"He's not wearing any pants," I giggled and gave the stereoscope back to her.

"And look at this one," she told me. "It's from Oregon."

"Oregon? Oh, let me see."

I was shocked to see the image of a man being attacked by a big bear.

"'In the Wilds of Oregon,'" I read at the bottom of the card.

"Doesn't that look exciting?" I asked Harriet. But from the look on Harriet's face, I could see she didn't think so.

"Girls," Mr. Fancher called. "We can have our Christmas now," he announced.

"Do you have a real Christmas?" I asked.

"Usually," Harriet explained. "When Mama was alive, we always had Christmas with a tree and presents. This year it's not gonna be the same but Pa has planned a big surprise," she said, pulling me off the sofa.

Mr. Fancher stood in front of the door between the hallway and the parlor. An old, tattered sheet had been hung about waist high across the frame. Mr. Fancher held a bamboo fishing pole in his hand.

"Could I interest anyone in going fishing?" he asked.

"Me, me," Harriet and I both cried out.

"Company should go first," he said and handed me the pole. He motioned for me to put the hook over the edge of the sheet and see if I got any bites. I let my line fall over the other side and before long, it felt like a big old catfish was tugging and tugging on the line.

"Well, pull it up, girl," Mr. Fancher said. There, hooked to the end, was an orange, nice as you please, tied all around with string and the hook secured through one of the strands.

Harriet hooked herself an orange. Mr. Fancher even got Marie Louise to join us. Then it came my turn again and this time I brought up a small box.

"C-R-A-Y-O-L-A," I spelled on the lid. "What is this?" I asked.

"They're called crayons, Callie," Mr. Fancher explained. He knelt down and opened the box's lid for me. "And they're for drawing."

"Look, I've gotten some, too," Harriet squealed as the string of her pole flipped up, dangling another box of crayons off the end.

"Oh, thank you, thank you," I said. "Are they expensive, Mr. Fancher?" I asked.

"No, not really," he answered. "Only nine cents."

"Callie! Manners, manners, manners. Where are your manners?" I heard from behind the curtain. "To ask the price is not polite," we heard Opa say.

Harriet pulled back an edge of the curtain. "So you're the big fish," Harriet said. Opa turned red and ducked down behind the curtain once again.

Marie Louise caught two lovely mother-of-pearl haircombs. We fixed them in her hair. She sat in the seat by the window the rest of the afternoon, reaching up to touch them once in a while.

Harriet and I were each given a piece of paper. I drew a picture of Harriet and me under the linden tree having our picnic, the way we did the day of the threshing dinner. I put in our dolls, Rose and Victoria Isabella, and Harriet and me in our best dresses. I drew a bright checkered blanket and put lots of food out. I made the sunshine all yellow and golden up in one corner. As I was filling in the blue sky, Opa said we needed to get started home.

We offered our reluctant good-byes. I knew we would be heading straight home, since the snow was beginning to stick and had already spread a fine white covering like meringue all over the countryside. The snow was even getting deep enough to hide the corn stubble in the fields.

When we pulled away from Fanchers' barnyard, I stuck a mittened hand out from under the blanket and waved. "Good-bye and thank you one million six hundred thousand times," came out in a breathy cloud. "Do you believe we have an orange?" I asked Opa about halfway home. I held it in my hand and kept sniffing the wonderful scent.

"Here, Opa," I said and put the orange under his nose, "doesn't it smell as good as Paris perfume?"

"Ja, it is our good fortune to have such nice neighbors. And I think I am so lucky to have you and Katherine so healthy. I see Marie Louise and my heart, it aches."

"Once Katherine gets home, we'll share our orange," I said, already thinking about how we would savor each juicy section. The last time we had oranges was nearly a year earlier, since they were so expensive and such a special treat.

When we turned onto Mule Barn Road, I noticed a set of wagon tracks already in the snow.

"Wonder who's out on an evening like this?" I asked Opa.

It wasn't until we neared our farm that I felt my heart skip a beat. I saw the tracks turn down our lane. Snow was falling so hard it was difficult to see the house clearly, but the tracks in the snow were fresh.

They led right into our barn. We pulled up alongside the big doors. Fanny shook the snow from her mane the minute we stopped. Opa slid the long doors open. We saw Uncle Mike's wagon inside with Blick still standing in his harness and all in a lather. Uncle Mike's voice startled us from the darkness.

"Help me, Johannes," was all he said, but I saw him kneeling in the wagon. He lifted a body wrapped in blankets into his arms. "We've got to get her into the house where it's warm."

Opa helped Uncle Mike with the bundle. I ran ahead and held the door for them. They laid the person carefully on the table. Not until I struck the match for the kerosene lamp and the flame spurted up, did I realize the body on the table belonged to my sister, Katherine.

CHAPTER SIXTEEN

Models of Fashion

Seeing Katherine like that was almost like seeing Mama dead all over again. "Is Katherine gonna die?" I asked. "Does she have diphtheria? Don't let her die, Opa."

"We'll put her in Elschen's room," Opa said, as Uncle Mike picked Katherine up to move her. The picture that came to my mind was Mama and the evening she'd died with the baby in her arms in that same room.

Katherine's clothes were soaked and her feet were covered in slush and mud nearly up to her ankles. Her beautiful auburn hair lay in caked clumps with stones and mud mixed together where her head had rested on the ground.

"She was where?" Opa asked Uncle Mike. Uncle Mike was unfolding a quilt from the trunk.

"Harold Comstock found her collapsed on the Old Post Road coming in from Noblesville. She came to for a while and told him she was walking home for Christmas."

Opa tucked the blankets around her sides.

"She said to Harold that she'd quit her job, cooking for Mary. Said she wouldn't go back there if it was the last job on earth."

Opa took off his coat and rolled up his sleeves.

"Ach," Opa muttered. "I tell you, Michael, diese Frau ist schrecklich! Never again will she come near my family." Opa touched Katherine's cheek with his hand.

"She's chilled clear through to the bone," Uncle Mike said. He leaned over and picked at the mud and laces to get her shoes untied. He gently worked each shoe off, then peeled her socks down. He drew back in horror. Blisters the size of quarters were covering the soles and arches of her feet. The bottoms of her shoes were worn through in two or three places. Any little spot where leather could rub had left a red mark or a swollen circle of raw, bleeding skin.

"Do you want me to go get Doc Taylor?" Uncle Mike asked.

"Nein," Opa replied. "I think we can nurse her back to health on our own." He began the work of getting Katherine's wet clothes off.

"Wir brauchen Zwiebeln!" he said, without looking at Uncle Mike.

"The onions are in the pantry. The frying pan's on top of the dry sink," I explained.

I helped Opa with Katherine's shirt. As we pulled it off her arms, we saw a fiery rash running along her shoulders and up into her hairline.

"Opa, look," I cried. I bit my lip and felt my stomach turn. I lifted up a clump of her hair and quickly let go.

"She's covered in nits," I told him. He only shook his head, then began giving orders.

"Go get the kerosene, Callie. Tell Michael to put the kettles on the stove and warm up the kitchen so it feels like we are baking bread." I was already halfway out the room when he called to me. "And bring in the sheep dip, off the huckster we bought."

By the time I returned, Katherine's clothes were in a pile in a corner of the room. I helped Opa get the big chunks of mud off her face with a washcloth. Her lips were dry and cracked along the edges.

"Die Zeitung, Callie, die Zeitung," Opa called, and I went searching in the parlor for the newspaper. I came back and spread it on the floor where Opa pointed, helping him move Katherine to the edge of the bed.

"You hold her," he told me. I watched as he took a pair of Mama's sewing shears.

"No, Opa," I said, "you can't do that."

"But we must." He held up a clump of Katherine's hair.

"Opa, you can't cut off her hair," I cried.

Opa answered me by pulling the clump a little higher and cutting it only two or three inches from Katherine's scalp. Each heavy strand fell onto the newspapers, making a crinkling sound. After he had cut the long strands away, he took a pocket comb and held up the other sections and cut them so that her hair was only an inch or two long all over. I couldn't help but start to cry.

Opa took a small rag and soaked it with kerosene. He dabbed Katherine's head with the awful smelling stuff. She winced with pain. I knew the kerosene on the raw nit bites would burn like fire. After Opa had soaked Katherine's scalp completely, he took the comb and worked it through the short stubble. I held Katherine's head nearly suspended over the edge of the bed. With every draw of the comb, we heard a sound like rain falling on the newspaper. It was nits, though. Opa was combing hundreds of nits out of Katherine's hair, and they were raining down on the pages of the *Prairie Farmer*.

After we'd soaked and combed Katherine's hair one more time, we moved a bucket of sheep dip under her head and rinsed everything with the tarry smelling mixture.

"We'll bathe her now," Opa told me and Uncle Mike. Somehow the three of us managed to get her into the bathtub. Opa had me do the washing. I nearly cried with I saw the nit bites all over her shoulders and buttocks. I washed her the same way I'd seen mothers wash a little baby, gently cleansing her face while I supported her head. I made sure her feet were clean and the mud washed out of the blisters. The warm water seemed to revive Katherine a little. Opa kept adding hot water every now and again from the big silver tea kettle. Uncle Mike had done a good job of making the room warm enough to bake a dozen loaves of bread. By the time I had finished giving Katherine a bath, the whole house smelled of frying onions.

We used a heavy flannel sheet for a drying towel and sat her in the rocking chair. Uncle Mike doctored her feet with salve and put on a pair of clean white, cotton socks. She looked so sad with her hair sticking out every which way. We stripped the bed and put all the clothes and bedding on the back porch. Katherine was conscious enough to try and get one of Mama's nightgowns on, and I took a towel to pat her hair dry. It stuck out on her head like a porcupine. I gently combed her hair. She looked just like a boy. I held back my tears.

"Oh, Katherine." I held her limp body close to mine. The three of us helped get her into bed. I tucked her in and held her hand. She looked at me and called my name.

"Merry Christmas," she whispered, "I'm so glad to be home."

Opa brought in an onion poultice wrapped in bed sheeting.

"To keep the lungs clear and keep away Lunge-nentzündung."

"Pneumonia? Do you think she's gonna get pneumonia?" I asked.

"That is what the poultice will keep away," Opa explained. We put the warm poultice on her chest. She lay there still and quiet. Opa shooed me out of the room and told me I was next.

I knew after handling Katherine's hair and all the nits, I would have to take my turn in the tub. I emptied the dirty water and filled the tub with clean water from the stove. The snow had stopped and the night was crisp and clear. The stars fairly jumped out of the sky, they were so bright. I stared up at Orion's Belt as it sparkled and twinkled.

"Katherine's home," I announced. "We've got her back home now and everything's gonna be fine," I said with confidence.

Opa was exhausted. He sat with me in the kitchen while I took my bath. He made sure I scrubbed from the top of my head to the very tips of my toes. When it was time for the sheep dip, he made me dunk my head into the bucket twice.

Wrapped in a clean towel, I stood by the kitchen window and watched Uncle Mike take the pile of bedding and Katherine's clothes out to the middle of the yard. He dumped them on the ground, doused them with kerosene and set them on fire. As I put on fresh drawers and my nightgown, Uncle Mike quickly walked back toward the house. The door opened. I knew why he had been in such a hurry to come in. The stench of burning hair filled the air.

By Tuesday, Katherine was able to take a little warm soup broth and by Friday, she could sit up a bit. We cooked special things to build up her appetite. For New Year's Day, I made Knee Patches, her favorite cookies. The whole house smelled of cinnamon and spices and flaky, fried dough. Katherine was as thin as a rail, and we worked hard to put some meat back on her bones. If we asked about Aunt Mary, Katherine would only say she was never going back there, ever again. In less than a week, the rash had calmed itself down enough so that it looked like fine pink freckles. On Saturday, Katherine asked for the mirror on Mama's dresser.

"My hair, my hair," she sobbed. "Oh, please Callie, you mustn't look at me. I'm so ugly." She tried to hide her face under the covers or put her arm over the top of her head.

"It's gonna grow out, Katherine," we tried to tell her. "Give it a little time. It'll grow out."

The following Saturday, Uncle Mike came out again. This time, he had a surprise for Katherine. He walked right into the bedroom and sat down on the edge of her bed, still wearing his hat and coat.

"Now this here's a surprise for you, Katherine. When I saw this magazine, I said to Harold Comstock, I'm gonna have to take that to Katherine." He pulled a magazine out from underneath his coat. "It's one of them fashion magazines, Katherine. And the reason I got it is because of the women and their haircuts." Uncle Mike was flipping through the pages and leaning so Katherine could see the pictures.

"Now lookee here," he pointed. "Don't that beat all. Paris fashion, it says here, and look at their hair. Sort of slicked back the way yours is and short like yours, too. Why, a person would think you were right straight from Paris, France, with that new haircut of yours."

Katherine took the magazine from him and studied the pictures.

I took every comb I could find from the top of Mama's dresser and the ribbons from her sewing basket. I sat in the middle of the bed with Katherine, and we tried to make Katherine's hair look like the latest fashion from France. We fixed combs and made finger waves along the tops and sides. Katherine's green eyes looked twice as big. After every new style, she'd hold up the mirror. Finally she said in despair, "It's no use, Callie, I look like a boy," and she hid her face in the pillow. That's when I thought of what I needed to do, while Katherine took her afternoon rest.

Katherine screamed when she saw me.

"Gott im Himmel, Gott im Himmel," Opa kept saying.

The whole process had gone very quickly. I'd done exactly what I'd seen Opa do to Katherine. I'd taken the comb, pulled up a shock of hair and cut if off about two or three inches from my scalp, the same way he'd done. My headful of muddy brown curls lay in a heap on the floor beside Mama's sewing basket.

I hadn't used a mirror, but from all the commotion, I could tell my new haircut must've turned out worse than I thought. At first Opa looked angry and then he looked as though he might laugh.

"Come here, mein Herzchen," he said to me.

I walked over to him, and he put his arms around me. He held up the fashion magazine and looked from me to Katherine and back to the magazine. "Now I have two models of fashion," he said. "And they come all the way from Paris to live with their opa. Such a lucky grandfather I am." He winked as he spoke.

I didn't bother correcting him. Instead I simply locked my arms around his neck and gave him a big hug. Later that evening, Katherine got out of bed and came into the kitchen to eat her favorite dinner, tomato dumplings.

"Sit over here," she ordered after the dishes were cleared away. She ran her fingers through my shorn locks.

"What are you gonna do?" I asked.

"Try to even it up," she explained. "Next time, don't play so fast and loose with the shears, Calista Marie."

I sat on a tall stool in the middle of the kitchen with a towel around my shoulders while Katherine snipped and clipped at my fuzzy hair.

"Fashion models, my foot," she muttered. "I still think we look like two boys."

CHAPTER SEVENTEEN

So Glad You're Home

The weather turned raw and nasty the next few weeks, and we were housebound. A bright red cardinal, chirping from the bushes by the kitchen door, was our only caller. The roads were so rainy and muddy that Uncle Mike missed one of his Saturday visits. The cold seemed to bother Opa's breathing, and Katherine took to chilling the minute she went more than ten feet away from the stove. So, we all stayed put, like three ticks on a bear's back on a blizzardy winter's day.

Gradually, Katherine's and Opa's strength returned and my nursing duties eased up. I shared my crayons with Katherine. We drew picture after picture until each waxy stick was only a small nub. There were as many books at our house as fingers on one hand. Not counting Opa's Bible, which was written in German, and a book of farm calculations, there were three others; my Alexander speller, which only had words, *Robinson Crusoe*, and *Little Women*. When Katherine was still getting her strength back, I read to her. Some days, I'd read as many as fifteen or twenty pages. During the exciting parts, I'd get to going back and forth so fast in the rocker I nearly went over backward. Once Katherine jumped off the bed and caught me by the ankles in the nick of time.

When Katherine was finally allowed to come out into the parlor, I read her the part about Robinson Crusoe's shipwreck. Playacting the brave Crusoe himself, I held the book in my left hand and climbed up on the sofa in my stocking feet. The davenport became my sinking ship. I cringed and rolled with the raging sea. Waves crashed down upon me time and time again. Undaunted, I struggled to my feet. I landed flat on my stomach as I read about being dragged twenty feet under, then bounced back to the top, gasping for air, strangling and choking on salt water. I was being pummeled by the crushing force of the waves.

Katherine's eyes grew bigger and bigger as she watched my every move.

"A rock, a rock," I shouted. I clung to the overstuffed end of the couch. The wave abated. I stood up, arms flung out. Coughing, sputtering, gasping for breath, ready to make my mad dash to the safety of the shoreline.

"Young lady," Opa asked sternly, "was machst du?"

"Nothing, Opa," I muttered as I collapsed into an embarrassed heap by the end of the sofa and tried to hide behind my overstuffed rock.

"Callie," Katherine said as she kept her finger on a spot in *Little Women*, "listen to this part." She read me all about Jo and how her hair had been singed so badly from the curling irons that it had to be cut off.

"Jo's hair turned out frizzled," she explained. "They tied a ribbon round her head, and she didn't look so much like a boy. Do you suppose we could do that, too?"

We looked in Mama's sewing basket and found a length of wide blue grosgrain ribbon. I tied it around Katherine's head, making a neat bow on top.

"You look fine," I told her, combing through one of the waves. Even Uncle Mike thought the ribbon looked very fashionable when he came out on his next visit. The color and shine in Katherine's auburn hair had come back, and though her haircut was painfully short, her hair was still the same beautiful color.

About a week later, snow cushioned the sound of

wagon wheels. Pounding on the kitchen door was the first we knew of a visitor coming into the yard. With Katherine in the parlor on the sofa and me in the rocking chair beside her, there was no place for her to hide as Opa pulled the door open and Bert Goodner stepped inside the house.

He made polite conversation with Opa for a minute or two, and then Bert walked into the parlor and right over to Katherine. I saw how horrified she looked, there on the sofa in one of Mama's old dresses, all bedded down with quilts, her hair so short and stubbly.

Bert stood there, towering over both of us, his hat in his hands and snow still on his boots.

"Your uncle Mike came over yesterday and told me you were home again. Told me what a hard time you'd had. I thought maybe something was wrong when I didn't hear from you the last few months."

Katherine looked up. She put both her hands up to her hair. "Oh, Bert," she said, "my hair . . . I look . . ." she started to say.

Bert sat down on the edge of the sofa by Katherine's knees.

"Now don't you go worrying about your hair, Katherine. Your uncle Mike told me about that, too. I just came out here to tell you that I've been worried sick about you. I've thought about you every day and prayed you were all right. Well, mercy, to see you sittin' here now, why that does my heart so much good. You're a sight for sore eyes."

I watched as the words tumbled out of the big man.

"I didn't come out here to stay. I only came out here to make sure with my own eyes that your health is better." He stood up quickly.

"Oh, Bert, I look so awful . . ." Katherine said. She buried her face in her hands.

He leaned down and gently took one of her hands and held it in his.

"Now listen here, Katherine," he said, kneeling on one knee. He tipped her chin up with his other big hand. "You look like an angel to me. Just like an angel on one of them store-bought postcards."

He reached into his pocket and pulled out a small package tied in twine.

"I thought you might be able to use these," he said. As Katherine opened the package, length upon length of colorful ribbons tumbled out. Reds, greens, plaids, polka dots.

"Oh, thank you Bert," she said, giving him a hug around the neck. "It's awfully sweet of you."

Bert looked a little embarrassed.

"Guess I'd better be goin'," he said, then pointed to me. "You take good care of your big sister, Callie, you hear?"

"Yes sir," I replied, feeling like I should stand at attention after hearing his order. He stood up and said a few things to Opa, then left nearly as quietly as he'd come. I watched him go until his buggy turned down the lane onto Mule Barn Road.

When I went in to tell Katherine he was gone, I found her sitting up, the ribbons all hooked through her fingers. She was crying in great big, gulping sobs.

"Why are you crying?" I asked. I couldn't understand. Bert had just come all the way out to see her, and he'd brought her a present, to boot.

In between sniffles, she finally managed to tell me, "I've never had anybody be so nice to me before, Callie. Never so nice as that."

Within a few minutes, we managed to tie every ribbon Bert had brought Katherine around her head. We laughed this time when she looked in the hand mirror, for she truly was a sight for sore eyes.

A February thaw started that perked up our spirits and allowed us to get out of the house for the first time in weeks. Katherine was feeling well enough for us to pull on pairs of old felt boots that had belonged to Mama and Papa. We walked out to the barn to see Fanny and Hester. We pushed the barn doors open in the back and stood there smell-

ing the clean, warm air and watching the snow melting and shimmering in the sunshine.

"I'm so glad you're home," I told her.

"Me, too," she answered.

"Why won't you talk about what happened at
Aunt Mary's?"

"I don't want to talk about it!"

"Why not?"

"I don't like to remember it. It was all so bad, I
couldn't even write home."

"Did you tell Opa what happened?"

"Only a little," Katherine said as she sat down on
a bale of straw.

"Was it that awful?"

"Most of it," Katherine said, nodding her head.
"Almost all of it."

"Aunt Mary nearly worked you to death," I said.

"Aunt Mary doesn't know anything else but work,
Callie. She's an old, bitter, miserly woman with
nothing in her life but hard, miserable, backbreak-
ing work." Katherine picked out a piece of foxgrass
from the straw and chewed on the end.

"How did you get the nits?"

Katherine looked up at me. "Promise me you
won't tell Opa?"

"I promise, cross my heart."

"My room in the attic was freezing, and I didn't

have enough blankets. The only other place to sleep was in a little alcove on a pallet behind the stove in the kitchen."

"On the floor? She made you sleep on the floor?"

"If I'd have been a boarder and paid her money, I suppose she'd have been nicer to me. But I was only the hired help. Aunt Mary treats the hired help no better than a dog. At night I'd pull a rug over me for extra warmth, and it was the rug the dog slept on during the day. I did that at first, but then I had to start sleeping back in the attic."

"What do you mean at first?"

Katherine looked at me. "Remember, you promised not to tell."

"All right, I won't breathe a word of what you say."

"I did that until Mr. Montgomery, one of the boarders, started coming into the kitchen at night."

"What did he want in the kitchen at night?"

"Well, to be honest, the first time he came down, I think he really and truly wanted something to eat. But then he started appearing regularly. Instead of getting something to eat, he'd talk to me."

Katherine stood up and looked out the barn door, still holding the foxgrass in her hand.

"The first time or two, he only talked to me, real nice and friendly like. But then he asked me to come sit on his lap. Said it was more comfortable than the floor. When I wouldn't, he got ugly and mean. He said awful things to me."

"What did you do?"

"Well, the first night, I hid in the outhouse because there was a lock on the door from the inside. But I was so cold I thought I'd freeze to death." Katherine turned away, and I walked over and put my arm around her.

"It's all right," I told her. "There's no call to talk about this if you don't want."

"I guess it won't hurt," she replied. "Talking to you about it is making me feel better. The next day," she explained, "I found extra blankets in a chest in one of the bedrooms. I hid them away up in the attic. I'd sneak up the back stairs of a night and hide in there. I pushed a chair up against the door so no one could come in. But I could hear him. He was a sneaky weasel, he was. He'd come up those back stairs all quietlike. But I could hear him breathing heavily and trying to push on the door real gently with his shoulder." Katherine shuddered and I rubbed her arm.

"You cold?"

"No, not cold, but thinking about it all over again kind of gives me the shakes. Then that last night," she went on, "I didn't get the chair propped up good in front of the door. He got the door open a little, but I was ready for him. I'd found me a two-by-four and put it by the door. When his hand pushed through the door, I hit it with that board as hard as I could swing."

"Katherine, you did that?" I asked, absolutely amazed.

"You bet I did, Callie," she said, looking straight at me. "When Aunt Mary got wind of what happened the next morning, she took a belt to me. She said I acted awful toward one of her boarders, and he'd left without paying his rent. When she said she was gonna take his rent out of my wages, I told her I quit. Q-U-I-T. I wasn't gonna work for her anymore."

"Oh, Katherine," I said, hugging her, "I'm glad you left there. What an awful place. Aunt Mary didn't seem like that when she was around Mama."

"Well, Callie, I don't care if Aunt Mary is family or not. She and Mama were the only ones in the family to ever get along. I still don't know how we're gonna have enough money to get us through the winter, but I'd rather eat sauerkraut and potatoes every day and make my clothes out of old rags than work for Aunt Mary again."

"I don't blame you."

"But, Callie, you've got to promise me," Katherine said. She held me by the shoulders as she spoke. "Don't ever tell a soul what I just told you. Never. Ever."

"All right, I promise. Cross my heart."

In the early evening, we played checkers in the parlor while Opa smoked his pipe.

"I think you are well enough now to sleep in the upstairs, Katerina?"

"Oh yes, Opa. I'm fine now. I'd much rather be upstairs with Callie," Katherine answered.

"Then we put you up the stairs tonight again," he said as he sat tipping back and forth in the rocking chair.

"To bed, to bed now," he told us. "Up the stairs I come in a minute to tuck you in."

Katherine and I made our last trip to the outhouse. I waited my turn by the door for her, then we raced all the way into the house and up the stairs. It was so good to have the old Katherine with me again.

We washed our faces in the basin and slid our nightgowns over our heads and hopped into bed. We sat up next to each other and propped our pillows behind our backs. We heard Opa's heavy footsteps on the stairs, his cane thumping with every step.

"What do you hear, Katherine?" I said loudly and fluttered the covers. Suddenly a growling, grizzling, grumping sound was coming from the stairwell. Katherine looked at me and smiled.

"A bear!" she screamed.

"A bear!" I screamed. We dove under the covers together.

The grumbling, shuffling bear came into the bedroom.

"Little girls," it growled, "so hungry I am for tasty little girls."

Opa grizzled and growled and beat on the covers with his hands. We screamed and cried out.

"So hungry I am for legs," the bear said loudly. He grabbed onto my arm.

"Opa, you've got my arm!" I shouted.

"Then so hungry I am for arms tonight," the bear replied. I felt the bear grab my arm and make eating noises. I started screaming even louder.

The growling and grizzling suddenly stopped. We lifted back the covers. Opa was sitting on the edge of the bed. He was huffing and puffing and all red in the face. His fuzzy white hair stood on end all over his head.

"Do you need a heart pill?" I asked.

"Nein," he answered, supporting himself with his hands on his knees.

"Such an old bear I am to be house roughing."

Katherine and I giggled even louder.

Opa turned to look at us.

"Back to front again, I have it, don't I?" he asked.

"Yes, Opa," Katherine told him, giving him a kiss on the forehead, "but we still love you."

We straightened out the covers and laid down. Opa sat beside Katherine on the edge of the bed.

"I am liking your fashion model hair more and more," he said, brushing a wave off Katherine's forehead and springing out one of my curls.

"A little mouse has run into your room," he said to both of us. He took Katherine's arm and walked two fingers up to her shoulder as he spoke.

"Kommt eine Maus die Treppe rauf."

"A mouse comes up the stairs," Katherine and I repeated, the way we always had done with Mama.

"Klopft an. K-nock, k-nock, k-nock." Opa continued, tapping three times on Katherine's forehead.

"Anybody home?" we asked.

Opa wiggled Katherine's ear. "Klingelingeling."

"Ring, ring, ring goes the bell," we said. Then he tapped Katherine's nose.

Opa was quiet for a minute, watching the two of us sitting up in bed.

"I look at you both," he said, touching my cheek and running his hand along Katherine's head, "and it fills my heart so. I see your mother's smile, Katherine, in your face. And in you, Callie, I see your mother's sparkle. Her love for life. You are such a comfort to your old opa," he said, kissing us both on the forehead.

"Gute Nacht, meine Katerina. Gute Nacht, meine Callie," he said quietly. "Gute Nacht, meine Liebchen," we heard as he shuffled down the stairs.

CHAPTER EIGHTEEN

Questions, Questions, Questions

Late one Sunday afternoon, Katherine and I worked in the barn with Opa. The day was unusually warm, smelling and feeling like spring tornado weather. After we finished with our chores, we kept Opa company. Katherine played with the kittens, dragging pieces of string in a circle, while I kept busy straightening the tackle. Katherine and I climbed up into the hayloft. We let the doors fly open on both sides. From our spot, we could see clear around for miles. Dark storm clouds were moving in from the west. A strong gust of cool wind came up from nowhere and left goose bumps on our arms. We scooted a bale of straw over to our newly made window and watched as the storm moved across the sky. Lightning crackled along the horizon. We took turns counting the seconds from the thunder to see how many miles away the lightning was.

From our spot, up so high, we could see most of

Mule Barn Road before the rise by Fanchers' place. Katherine noticed the dust cloud first.

"There's a wagon coming," she said, holding her finger steady so I could trail my eye off the end to see where she was looking.

"Must be Uncle Mike," I said.

"He came yesterday," Opa added, overhearing us. He was standing by Fanny's stall in the middle section of the barn.

"Whoever it is, he'll have to hurry to beat the rain," Katherine told him.

We watched a line of rain follow behind the wagon, then catch up with it. As the wagon turned down the lane, everything began to glisten.

"There are two," I heard Katherine say. Both of us were intently staring out the barn door. "One's Uncle Mike."

"The other one's . . ." I whispered, but didn't finish. Slickers and wide-brimmed hats covered their faces. We knew for sure Uncle Mike would be driving Blick. The rain and wind caught the wagon full force as they headed straight toward the barn. Both riders had their heads down and their faces shielded.

Katherine and I hung over the edge of the loft and watched as Uncle Mike pulled the wagon through the big doors. Their slickers sparkled in the light.

"We almost made it," Uncle Mike said with a laugh. The other man was shaking off the wetness. It wasn't until he took off his hat that I realized the other man was Papa.

"Papa," I cried, nearly tumbling down the steps of the hayloft. "Papa, Papa, you're back." As he stepped down from the wagon, I ran into his arms, my face plastered against the wet slicker. Katherine was close behind me.

"Papa! Papa!" I exclaimed. The familiarity of his hug. The way he lifted me off my feet. It was all so wonderful.

I turned to see Uncle Mike watching me with a smile.

"He's back," I said to Uncle Mike, as though he couldn't see. "Papa's back."

Papa took off his slicker and threw it on the wagon. Katherine and I hugged him over and over again.

"Let me see you," he said, carefully holding each of us at arm's length for inspection. "You've grown so much Katherine," he announced. "You're such a young woman now."

"That I am, Papa," she answered.

"And my Callie?" he asked. "Are you so grown-up? Are you so different?"

"Yes sir," I answered. "Yes, Papa."

Papa looked us both up and down, not knowing what to say.

"And you look different, too," I told him. I ran my hand over his smooth, hairless face.

"Yes," he replied, "I guess I do."

"Look, Opa," I said as I turned around, "Papa's back." I glanced around the barn, but there was no Opa. "Opa?" I called out.

Uncle Mike was easing Blick out of his harness. "Your opa's gone into the house," I heard him say. I saw Opa's huddled figure through the kitchen window.

"We can wait out the storm here in the barn," Papa said. The three of us stood by the door and watched the rain come down in sheets.

I'd hoped for this moment, having Papa home, for so many months.

"You know about Mama, don't you?" Katherine asked.

"Yes," he replied and put his hand on her shoulder. "Pastor Greene got word to me when she died."

"When was that?" I asked.

"September," was all he said. "I'm sorry with all my heart for what happened." Papa held us tight. "I'm as sorry as I can be. But life has to go on."

"Why did you wait so long to come get us?" I questioned.

"I was busy," was all he said. "I was making arrangements for a farm," he explained. "Doesn't sound as though you received any of my letters."

"No, Papa," I said quickly. I looked at Katherine and realized I'd never told her about the other letters from Papa that Opa had burned in the stove. I stared at Papa as he spoke.

"Have you come to take us back to Oregon?" I wanted to know.

"Yes," Papa replied.

"Soon? Will we go soon?"

"Probably."

"How soon?"

"In a few days," he answered.

"Oh, that soon," Katherine replied.

"I didn't know until a week ago that I was coming," Papa told us. "I wasn't sure I could get away."

The rain let up a little, and we made a dash for the porch. We stood shaking off the wetness for a few seconds before we went inside.

"Did you find us a farm?" I asked.

"I sure did," he said. "I found us a beautiful farm so close to the ocean you could stand on the front porch, throw a rock, and hear the splash."

"Did you buy a farm?" I wanted to know, wondering how he'd suddenly gotten the money back. I wanted to ask about the man who had swindled him in St. Louis, and what had really happened with Opa's money.

"Now don't you go worrying your pretty head about business things," he told me.

"I was just wondering . . ." I started to say.

"What's there to wonder about? Your papa's taken care of everything."

"Oh, Papa, that's nice. You buying a farm out in Oregon and all. It's the way you and Mama planned it. She'd be so pleased," Katherine said.

"And if you've still got a mind to, Katherine, you could teach school out there. We need schoolteachers. I heard tell they could use teachers in Tillamook."

I didn't say anything. I watched Papa as he hugged Katherine and patted me on the back.

"Well, maybe it's time to go in and face your grandfather. How is he anyway?" Papa asked Katherine. "Still as cross as an old bear?"

"Oh, Papa," Katherine said, "you know that's only gonna make things worse if you talk like that." Papa kept his arm around Katherine as they opened the door and went into the house. I stayed a few paces back. I didn't have the heart to keep up with them. My mind was churning and churning. There were too many things that didn't make sense.

Why wouldn't Papa answer my questions? Had he really taken Opa's money? Maybe he didn't want us to know about being swindled by the man in St. Louis. How could he buy a farm if he didn't have any money? I stood on the porch a minute, hoping a long, deep breath would clear my mind. I thought, too, it might help the queasy feeling that was coming over me. I couldn't put my finger on what it was that made me think it, but I had a sinking feeling in the pit of my stomach that Papa was lying right through his teeth.

The smell of frying bacon filled the room as we entered the kitchen. Opa was making supper.

"Opa, Papa's back," Katherine announced.

"Johannes," I heard Papa say. "Hello there, Johannes."

"Ja, I see you," Opa replied, without turning around.

"Well, aren't you gonna say hello?" Katherine asked.

Opa turned with the spatula in his hand and looked Papa square in the face.

"Hello, Owen," was all he said, then looked back at the stove.

*   *   *

All during supper I found myself staring at Papa. He talked so big and loud about Oregon, telling us all about the farm and the land.

"Why, we have trees on our property so big you can't get your arms around them," he boasted. "And ferns growing wild in the woods all year round. Everything's so lush and green."

Papa kept up a conversation for all of us. Opa didn't say much, so it was Uncle Mike and Katherine who quizzed Papa about his trips back and forth.

"I came on the train this time," he told us. "Train travel is the only way to go. Chooo-choooo," he pretended, like when I was a little girl.

Katherine and I cleared the table. Papa and Uncle Mike went out to the barn. Papa was bragging about the herd of fifty Holsteins at the new farm. Before Uncle Mike and Papa came back in, they stood on the back porch as Papa lit a cigarette, the first time I'd ever seen him smoke. While they sat in the parlor and talked, Katherine and I sat on the floor and played checkers. Opa turned in early. I brought out my ribbon from school and some of my best drawings to show Papa. I wanted to tell him all about being the representative for the spelling bee.

"Not now, Callie," he said, shooing me away. "Can't you see I'm busy talking with your uncle Mike?"

As the clock struck eight, I went over and stood by Papa and Uncle Mike until there was a space in their conversation.

"What is it, Callie?" Papa asked.

"Tomorrow, I could take you out to the cemetery," I offered. "I could show you where Mama is buried." Papa took hold of my hand.

"I suppose," he answered. "If you'd like that, it would be fine with me."

"In the afternoon, then, right after lunch," I told him.

Katherine and I put on our nightgowns and got ourselves ready for bed. We waited for Papa to come upstairs, but he never did.

"I guess he's not gonna come and tuck us in," I whispered to Katherine.

"Guess not."

"Do you think Papa seems the same?" I asked.

"Sure. He's still our father," she answered.

"He doesn't seem the same to me."

"How's that?"

"There's something different about him."

"Maybe you're the one that's different. Did you ever think of that?" Katherine tried to fluff up her pillow. "His beard's gone, and he smokes now," she added.

"Yes, but it's more than that."

I lay on my stomach and propped myself on my elbows so I could see her better.

"He hasn't asked anything about us. He didn't even notice how short our hair was."

"He's been gone, Callie. Things have been difficult for him. Things have changed. Heaven knows, you and I have changed. Give him time."

"He has all that talk about the farm. And he brags so big and boastful about Oregon."

"Well, maybe. But doesn't it sound absolutely wonderful?" Katherine interrupted.

"If I didn't know better, I'd think you bought it all, hook, line and sinker."

"What is there to doubt? I'm gonna have my first teaching job. We're gonna move out to a beautiful new place. We'll have nice things and more exciting places to go than you can shake a stick at. You could show a little more enthusiasm, Calista Marie."

"I'm not so sure about all of this as you are. I've got a lot of things rolling around in my head. Who does Papa mean when he always says 'we'?"

"For heaven's sake, that's only an expression," Katherine said. "Stop your worrying, Callie, and go to sleep."

I lay there, the most confused I think I'd ever been.

How could Papa buy a farm when he lost all the

money? Why didn't he come for us sooner if he knew in September that Mama died? Who was the "we" Papa kept talking about? And if the three of us left for Oregon, what would happen to Opa?

The questions rattled around in my head like a handful of marbles in the bottom of an empty bucket.

CHAPTER NINETEEN

Quiet as a Church Mouse

As the buggy jostled and bumped on the way to the cemetery, I tried to pluck up my courage to ask Papa my questions. Katherine had stayed home to pack and Opa was nowhere to be found when it was time to leave. Papa and I had gone alone.

"You're quiet as a church mouse," Papa said to me. "Does going to Mama's grave make you sad?"

"Yes," I answered. "Does it make you sad?"

"Yes, of course," he replied. "It makes me sad especially to think your mama died so young and the baby died, too. I was hoping for a boy. We were hoping the move out to Oregon would give us a clean start. A farm of our own. A chance to have our own land."

"But you had that here."

"Not really. Opa only rents the farm." Papa turned to me. "You're gonna love it out there, Callie. Why, it's better than anything you could ever have in Indiana. It's greener, prettier."

I looked around us as we rode. The fields were seas of mud and long uneven rows of corn stubble. Papa was right. Indiana, in the dead of winter, wasn't much to look at, but give it two or three months and the fields would be green and lush.

We turned down the road to the cemetery. I could see the gate up ahead of us. I took a deep breath and figured now was as good a time as any to ask him. "How did you get the money to buy the farm?" I questioned.

Papa waited a long time before he answered me. "Have you been talking to your grandfather?"

"No," I answered honestly.

"Somehow, young lady, I don't think I need to talk about my private finances with you."

"I know what happened in St. Louis," was all I said.

"I thought you said Mama didn't get my letters."

"She got that one, if that's what you want to know."

I showed Papa which path to follow as we pulled into the cemetery.

"It's straightened out now, Callie. I've handled everything. Don't worry your little head about it another minute." Papa tapped me on the knee like I was a little child.

I pointed to the grave marker where Mama was buried, and we stopped. Papa helped me jump down.

Elschen Kreuzer Common, I traced with my index finger as I knelt near the grave. Infant-Boy, it read below Mama's name. May 3, 1874–August 26, 1909. The headstone was plain and simple.

Papa didn't say anything and for some reason, I didn't have any tears in me.

"I wish you had come for us sooner," I whispered.

"I came as soon as I could, Callie. You know how hard it is to get away from fifty milking cows. Why, it's nearly impossible. We had to pay a hired hand to come and take care of them so I could leave. Every day I'm away, it's costing us money."

We got back in the wagon and rode through the rest of the cemetery to get turned around.

I held onto the edge of my cape and twisted the button at the throat round and round.

"Who's this 'we' you're always talking about?" I asked boldly.

"My, you're the curious cat today, aren't you?"

"Ever since you've been back, you keep talking about 'we' or 'us' every other sentence. Makes me curious who the 'we' is."

"There's already a family on the farm," he said casually.

"How can that be if you own it?"

"Well, it's part of the bargain."

"What bargain?"

"There you go again, asking too many questions. You're gonna worry your head off one of these days. I'll look over and see your head just rolling right along the road where it's plopped off from worrying too much about other people's business."

"Are these people gonna be there when we get there?"

"Certainly."

"Can't you tell them to leave?"

"I guess I could, but I don't want to." Papa looked at me long and hard. "Might be nice for you, Callie, there are children. You've always been so lonely out here, all by yourself. A couple of girls and a boy about your age. If you feel like you need to know, the farm was owned by a widow woman and I've taken it over. Her husband was killed last year in a logging accident."

"Do you work the farm for her?"

"You could say that."

"Is there a house? Is there room for us?"

"Certainly. You and Katherine will have to share. But there's plenty of room."

Things sounded a little too cozy. Then all of a sudden, a notion struck me.

"Are you gonna marry this woman? Well, are you, Papa?" I wanted to know. " 'Cause if you are, I can tell you now, I think it's wrong. Mama hasn't even been dead six months." I turned to look at him.

Papa looked away.

"Callie, I don't like the tone of your voice," he replied.

We were within sight of the farm, and I saw Opa and Uncle Mike walking out to the barn.

"What's gonna happen to Opa?" I asked as we turned down our lane.

"Don't know," Papa answered.

"He's got no place to go." We all knew Uncle Mike lived in the room above the dry goods store. There was only space for one person. "Can Opa come with us?"

"Callie, that's not for you to decide. That's up to Daisy and me."

"You and *Daisy*! Why would it matter to you and *Daisy*? Opa is family. He goes where we go."

"You're pokin' your nose into other people's business, Callie. You'd better watch your step."

As I stared at the empty fields and heard Papa's words echoing through my head, a thought hit me, as clear and true as if Papa had taken his hand and slapped me across the face with the idea.

"You've already married her, haven't you, Papa?" I accused. "Is that it? Well, tell me, Papa, have you?" He never answered me. As soon as we were into the yard, I jumped down from the wagon and ran over to the chicken coop. The words kept screaming in my head. Papa and Daisy! Papa and Daisy! Papa and Daisy! I leaned against the back wall. I felt sick inside, like I had a slithering snake crawling and churning around in my stomach. My head throbbed. The words hammered at my brain. Papa and Daisy. Papa and Daisy. The snake started twisting and turning in my chest. The words grew louder and louder, ringing in my ears. Papa and Daisy. Papa and Daisy. I started to sweat and held my stomach. Then before I could stop it, the snake was crawling in my throat, and I threw up all over the spirea bushes.

Katherine was a regular chatterbox at supper. She was caught up with what to take and what not to take. She'd packed everything from Mama's room and all my things, too. She was carrying on about some kind of trunk she'd come across in the attic when I broke my long silence.

"What about you, Opa?"

"What about me?"

"Are you gonna come with us tomorrow?"

Opa looked at Papa, then he looked back down at his plate again. "I was not asked," he said, without looking up.

"There's room for you, Johannes," Papa said. "Oregon's a lovely place. You take one look at those beautiful forests, and you'll be hooked. You get a whiff of that salt sea air, and you'll never want to go back to this old flat farmland again."

Opa scooted his chair back from the table and stood up. "This flat farmland, as you call it, has fed my family for forty years. Year after year, we have plenty to eat and clothes on our backs."

"Take it easy, Johannes, I wasn't lookin' for a fight here. I only wanted to make a point . . ."

"All yesterday and all today, you make your point. Talk, talk, talk. Oregon this and Oregon that. Such a place I have never seen. So maybe I cannot say that this Oregon is better. I ask myself, what would I need a better place for? Indiana and this farm. Have they not been good enough for Johannes Kreuzer? The people, here, I know. I trust. I know who it is that I am breaking bread with."

"And what does that mean?" Papa said, standing up very suddenly.

"If I stay, I will not break bread with a thief at every meal," Opa answered harshly.

"I didn't steal your money," Papa said.

"If you did not, then who did?"

"No one stole it. We agreed I could take it, remember?"

"I never said those words."

"Elschen told me . . ."

"How dare you bring Elschen into this."

"I'll bring her into it, if it's what's needed. Elschen took your money. She was the one who went out in the barn and dug it up."

I watched Opa. He looked as though someone had knocked the wind out of him. "My Elschen would never do that."

"Well, she's not here for us to ask, is she, Johannes?" Papa threw his napkin down on the table. His steps were hard and loud as he walked toward the door. "Don't ever accuse me of being a thief again."

Opa's face was red and flushed. He sank into his chair and put his hand up to his chest. He took a nitroglycerine tablet and put it under his tongue. Uncle Mike helped Katherine and me clear away the supper dishes.

The clock was striking nine, then ten, and Papa had not come in from the barn. Katherine and I

were getting ready for bed. The lid of our trunk
was still open for last-minute things.

"Do you suppose it gets cold in Oregon?" Katherine asked, holding up a heavy winter coat that had
belonged to Mama.

"Probably not as cold as it gets in Indiana," I
replied.

"I thought we should try and take as many of
Mama's things as we could."

I was glad to take Mama's things. They felt like
such a comfort to me. I watched Katherine pack
Mama's haircombs and a small packet of letters tied
round with a ribbon. Her favorite tatted hankies
and stockings were tucked into the lid of the trunk.

My mind was in such a jumble I could barely
keep up a conversation with Katherine. I couldn't
bring myself to tell her anything about the ride
back from the cemetery. What if it wasn't true about
Papa and Daisy? But then again, what if it was?
Mama wasn't even dead six months. Didn't Papa
love Mama? How could he do that? If he loved her,
how could he go and get himself married to another woman?

Opa didn't even tuck us into bed that night.
Katherine and I lay there, talking in the dark about

riding on a train and traveling all the way out to Oregon.

"The Pacific Ocean," I said out loud. "It doesn't sound half as exciting as it did at first."

Katherine sat bolt upright. "Why on earth would you say a thing like that?"

"Maybe it's 'cause I don't know where I'm going. When we get to Oregon, our lives are gonna be different. If we leave here, we'll leave behind all our memories," I said. "This is the only place I've ever known. What we know about Oregon you could put on the head of a pin. Besides, Oregon is so far away, we'll probably never get back to Indiana again."

Katherine gave me a look as though I'd lost all my marbles.

"Didn't you hear a thing Papa said?" she asked. "What's there to miss in Indiana? There's almost nothing in Indiana."

"Maybe for you and Papa, Katherine. But I like it here. There's this farm. There's Harriet. There's Fanny."

"Well, Oregon's got to be better for me. I'll have a teaching job. I'll be able to make money. We'll live on a beautiful farm. It's got to be prettier out there. Prettier. Greener. Indiana's only one old cornfield after another. Same as a freckle. If you've seen one, you've seen them all."

I turned away from her a little.

"Truth is, I don't want to leave. I wasn't meant to be some kind of world traveler. Maybe you are, but I'm not."

"Remember what Mama always said, Callie? It's true. 'It's a long, long road that has no turns.' " Katherine pushed my shoulder as she said it. "Well, if you stay here for the rest of your life, there won't be one single curve, one single bend in the road. Going out to Oregon is one new turn. All the way out to Oregon, a whole new life. This will be so exciting."

"One person's excitement is another person's misery," I recited, giving her another maxim.

Katherine blew out the candle on the nightstand. There was a long silence. I gave a big sigh.

"The real honest truth is, Katherine," I said softly, "I can't bear the thought of leaving Mama out here all alone. It feels like we're gonna forget all about her."

The brightness of the moon was coming in through the window. I could make out the trunk, sitting open at the end of the bed.

"We only got one Mama and she's buried here," I whispered. "Seems only fitting that we shouldn't leave her." Katherine fluffed up her pillow a bit as she stared out the window.

"Young children like us aren't supposed to bury their parents," I replied. "It's just not fair."

"Nothing's fair, Callie," Katherine answered. "People die when you don't mean for them to. Wars get started. Farms go bust and the land plays out."

"I wish with all my heart Mama hadn't gone and died," I said.

"I do, too," Katherine replied, putting her arm around me. "But our lives are gonna have to go on. Goin' out to Oregon was something Mama was gonna do herself. Seems like it won't hurt us to carry out her wishes."

Katherine was asleep in a few minutes. I lay there and thought about Mama. How she looked, how she smelled of rosewater. I tried to remember everything about her that I could. I was so afraid I'd forget what she looked like. I tried to remember how she wore her hair. The way her eyes were so green. The warm feeling of her arms around me. I wanted to make sure I took all those thoughts with me to Oregon.

Thoughts of Papa and Daisy crowded into my mind. I kept shoving them in the background.

You'll have to face Daisy and Papa when you get to Oregon, won't you, Callie? I told myself. I crawled to the end of the bed and looked at the stars.

"I won't forget you, Mama," I whispered to the open sky. "Cross my heart," I promised.

I could hear Opa's footsteps downstairs, pacing the length of the parlor. Every time I tried to keep my eyes shut tight, they popped wide open. I eased myself off the bed and started down the steps. I crouched low when I heard his voice getting louder and louder. I worked myself into a spot on the stairs where I couldn't be seen, but I could see out.

The only person in the room was Opa and he was carrying on a conversation with himself in German. Papers were scattered all over the credenza, and the ink and his favorite fountain pen were out.

I stood up and walked down the rest of the steps.

"Herzchen," Opa said with surprise, "it is so late. Why are you not asleep?"

"I couldn't sleep, Opa," I told him. I ran over and put my arms around his neck. I kept my face close to his and spoke.

"Are you coming with us, Opa?"

"Ah, mein Herzchen," he said slowly and leaned back in the chair, "a little I have been thinking on this."

"I want you to come with us," I pleaded. "I don't want to go unless you go."

"Yes, but you must go because you will be with your father," he reminded me.

"Please come with us," was all I could think to say again.

"All right, mein Herzchen, a little I will think on this." He kissed me on the forehead and turned me around and scooted me over to the stairs. "Like a little mouse," he told me, walking his fingers up my arm. "Steig die Treppe rauf!"

I tiptoed up the steps, but backtracked at the top. I crouched down and took tiny breaths as I hid a step or two above the landing. My heart was beating like a big bass drum.

I watched in silence as Opa knelt by the credenza and lifted back a corner of the rug.

I nearly gave myself away, for I gasped so loud. There in neat stacks were bills. Ones, fives, tens, and twenties. I watched Opa as he laid the money out on the table. He counted it all twice.

"What an old sly fox you are, Opa," I whispered. "You must have saved every single penny all winter."

He put the wad of money into his inside coat pocket. He moved the kerosene lamp over to the table and turned up the wick. He placed the bottle of black ink and the pen at the table and sat down. He opened up his Bible and began to write.

All the way across the room, I could hear his pen scratching the paper. When he'd finished writing, he placed his pipe and his pen in his satchel. He carefully tucked his Bible on top and closed the clasps. The clock on the mantel struck ten, and he looked up. I moved into the shadows and tiptoed all the way up the steps.

I climbed back into bed and lay there in the dark. My heart was pounding so hard, I thought it might burst. All I could do was whisper, "He's coming with us. He's coming with us."

CHAPTER TWENTY

Red Sky at Morning

Long before the sun cleared the horizon, Papa was calling to us.

"Get up, you sleepyheads, we're off to Oregon!" he hollered from downstairs.

Our lunch pails were packed and on the kitchen table. We were lucky. The day was clear and the weather was warm for February. While we dressed, I watched Uncle Mike bring Blick and the wagon out into the yard. Fanny and Hester were tied to the back with rope bridles.

We finished our packing and bumpity-bumped the trunk down the steps. Katherine carried one of Mama's sun hats. I wore one of her best bonnets. We made one last trip to the outhouse, and by the time we returned Papa had loaded the wagon.

"Wait, wait," I cried. I ran to the door one last time to fetch the clock from the mantel. "Can't forget this," I told Papa. He boosted me and Katherine up into the back of the wagon. We took our place on a bale of straw Uncle Mike had placed behind the wagon seat.

Opa pulled the kitchen door shut and put his satchel next to our bags. He lay his cane on the floorboards and hoisted himself onto the front seat next to Uncle Mike.

As we pulled away, I looked at the house and the yard. Another farmer would rent the place in a few months and make many changes. That morning, I tried to take it all in like a picture on one of those stereoscope cards. I wanted to remember the farm the way we'd had it. I pretended I was the photographer. A big puff of smoke went up as the camera took each photograph. Through the lens, I saw Mama sitting on the front porch in the rocker. Bert Goodner was singing there with Katherine on the steps. The attic window where I could see all the way to Fanchers' was there, too. I took in a little of the tulip tree and the springhouse. In another picture I saw the big red barn and the path out to the back fields of corn and wheat. Those sleek horses that pulled the threshing machine. The hill in back covered with hollyhocks, when it was summer.

*　　*　　*

We met Harriet and Orville Fancher at the end of our lane. They'd come to see us off and take Fanny and Hester to their farm.

"Good-bye," I called. "I'll write to you from Oregon." Harriet and her father waved. I tried to make a picture in my mind of them, too.

Blick took us into town, slow and steady. I looked at the long flat fields surrounding us. One cornfield after another. Katherine was right, but only about freckles. In a few more months, there would be cornfield after cornfield after cornfield. Row upon row of emerald green stalks. And there'd be wheat again. Acres and acres of golden wheat fields, dipping and waving in the breeze.

A flaming red sky was breaking across the horizon when we went through town. Uncle Mike stopped the wagon in front of the blacksmith's shop. Katherine hopped out and quickly ran over to the door of the little house beside the shop. She knocked loud enough to wake a dead person.

"Who's there?"

"It's me, Bert, Katherine Common."

The door flew open.

"We're leaving for Oregon," she announced. "We have to go right away to catch the train in Sheridan."

"Just like that?" we heard him ask.

I noticed he was standing there in his stocking feet, his shirt unbuttoned and his suspenders not even pulled up over his shoulders.

"Yes, just like that."

"Where're you going in Oregon? Will you be gone for good?" Bert stepped toward her. "Will I ever see you again?" he asked. He put his hands on her shoulders.

Katherine looked up at him. "I promise I'll write. You can come and visit me, if you'd like. Papa says there's a teaching post waiting for me," she replied.

"We're going to Tillamook!" I shouted. "That's T-I-L-L-A-M-O-O-K," I spelled, and Papa laughed.

Bert took Katherine in his arms and surrounded her with a hug. "You can count on it," he answered. I thought for a minute he was going to lift her off the ground. Instead he leaned his head down and kissed her square on the mouth, a deep, long kiss.

"Oh, Bert," Katherine said in surprise.

"He kissed her on the lips," I said to Opa in disbelief. "Did you see that? Right smack on the lips."

"Hush, Callie," Papa told me.

Bert walked with Katherine back to the wagon.

"Hello, or maybe I'd better make that good morning," Bert said to all of us. He scooped Katherine up in his arms and placed her on the bale of straw next to me. I was so thunderstruck, I couldn't even get my mouth open.

"Good-bye, Callie," Bert said to me. "You be sure and take care of your big sister for me until I get out to Oregon. Good-bye, now. All of you, have a safe trip."

"Auf Wiedersehen!" Opa called. Uncle Mike slapped the reins. We were off. Bert stood right in the middle of the road, waving to us until we couldn't see him any longer.

A ways out of town, we went past the cemetery. Uncle Mike slowed Blick down a bit. I thought about Mama and the baby. Big tears ran down my cheeks and dripped off my chin. Katherine put her arm around me, and I nestled into her shoulder. "We're only doin' what Mama would've done herself," Katherine said to comfort me. "Life has to go on."

"Good-bye, Mama," I whispered. "I promise I won't ever forget you. Cross my heart."

My eyes felt like they were stuck on that big old weeping willow tree where Mama was buried.

But I made myself turn around.

I draped my arms over Opa's shoulders and put my cheek up against his. I made myself look past Blick and past the fields surrounding us. I tried my hardest right then to look all the way out to Oregon. All the way out to the Pacific Ocean. I allowed myself to look back only once, at the willow tree.

Then we stopped at the crossroads. We were leaving Bakers Corner. On that February day, nineteen hundred and ten, we would leave Indiana. Papa slapped the reins over Blick's back, and the wagon jerked forward as we made the first turn down the long, long road to Oregon.

Glossary

Aufmachen, bitte!—Open up, please!

Auf Wiedersehen!—Till we meet again!

Dieb—thief

Dienstag—Tuesday

Diese Frau ist schrecklich!—That woman is
     dreadful.

Die Zeitung—the newspaper

Eintausend Kerzen—a thousand candles

Einundzwanzig, zweiundzwanzig, dreiundzwanzig,
     vierundzwanzig—twenty-one, twenty-two,
     twenty-three, twenty-four

Es braucht Zeit.—It takes time.

Für uns geht das Leben weiter ohne eure
     Mutti.—Life goes on (for us) without your
     mother.

Genug—enough

Gib es mir!—Give it to me!

Gott im Himmel.—God in Heaven.

Gute Nacht, meine Callie.—Good night, my
　　Callie.

Gute Nacht, meine Katerina.—Good night, my
　　Katherine.

Gute Nacht, meine Liebchen.—Good night, my
　　darlings.

Herzchen—sweetheart (an endearing term)

Himmel und Erde—Heaven and Earth (apples
　　and potatoes)

Hühnchen! Kommt her, meine
　　Hühnchen!—Chickens! Come here, my
　　little chickens!

Ich bin so müde.—I am so tired.

Ich weiss nicht.—I do not know.

Ja—yes

Ja, der Himmel war bewölkt.—Yes, the sky was
　　cloudy.

Klopft an. Klingelingeling.—Knocking. Ring,
　　ring, ring.

Kommt eine Maus die Treppe rauf.—A mouse
　　comes up the stairs.

Langsam!—Slowly!

Liebe, liebe—Dear, dear

Lumpenpuppen—rag dolls

Lungenentzündung—pneumonia

Meine gute, schöne Kuh.—My good, lovely cow.

Mein Kleines—my little one

Mein Liebchen—my darling

Mein Schatz—my treasure (another endearing
    term)

Mit Glöckchen—with bells on

Nein—no

Oh mein Gott! Oh mein Gott!—Oh my God! Oh
    my God!

Oma—Grandma

Opa—Grandpa

Sachte, sachte!—Be gentle!

Schlaf, Kindchen, schlaf.—Sleep, little one, sleep.

Schlange! Schlange!—Snake! Snake!

Schnitz und Knopfen—apples and buttons (dried
    apples and sausage slices)

Schrecklich! Schrecklich!—Dreadful! Dreadful!

Sehr gut—very good

Sie ist mein ein und alles.—She is everything to
    me.

Steig die Treppe rauf!—Climb up the stairs!

Tannenbaum—Christmas tree

Umlaut—modification of a vowel in the German
    language (as in a, o, u to ä, ö, ü)

Und in der Zwischenzeit—and between time

Vati—Papa

Verzeih mir.—Forgive me.

Viele Hunde sind des Hasen Tod.—With so
    many dogs, the rabbit has no chance.
    (There is no fighting against fearful odds.)

Vielen Dank!—Many thanks!

Vorsicht! Vorsicht!—Careful! Careful!

Was machst du?—What are you doing?

Wir brauchen Zwiebeln!—We need onions!

Zehn—ten

Zweiter Timotheus. "Denn ich werde schon
  geopfert und die Zeit meines Abscheidens
  ist vorhanden."—The Second Epistle of
  Paul the Apostle to Timothy, chapter four,
  verse six. "For I am now ready to be
  offered, and the time of my departure is at
  hand."